"Do you ever swim naked in the bay?" Colt asked.

"In the moonlight?" Annie asked.

"Yes."

"Do you read minds?" she asked. Only moments before, the image had inexplicably flashed through hers.

"No. I barely have time to read newspapers. You were thinking the same thing?"

"I don't want you to get the wrong idea," she said quickly.

"Don't worry. I've been called a rake and a Southern-fried Romeo, but never a cad." His grin was wicked.

"Thanks for the ice cream, Colt. I have to run; I have a million things to do."

"You didn't finish."

She gazed with longing at her dish. Laughing, Colt scooped up the whipped cream and cherries, and held the spoon to her mouth. How could she resist?

"You always save the best for last," he said.

"How did you know?"

"I do, too." He scraped the last bite from her bowl, then cupped her chin while she ate. She closed her eyes in sheer appreciation of the moment.

"Hmmm. . . . the last bite *is* always the best."

Suddenly she felt another touch, on her lips this time, whisper soft, gentle as dew falling on roses. Colt's lips on hers.

It was a brief kiss, so brief that when she opened her eyes she thought she might have dreamed it. Except for the gleam in his eyes. . . .

WHAT ARE *LOVESWEPT* ROMANCES?

They are stories of true romance and touching emotion. We believe those two very important ingredients are constants in our highly sensual and very believable stories in the LOVESWEPT line. Our goal is to give you, the reader, stories of consistently high quality that may sometimes make you laugh, sometimes make you cry, but are always fresh and creative and contain many delightful surprises within their pages.

Most romance fans read an enormous number of books. Those they truly love, they keep. Others may be traded with friends and soon forgotten. We hope that each LOVESWEPT romance will be a treasure—a "keeper." We will always try to publish

LOVE STORIES YOU'LL NEVER FORGET BY AUTHORS YOU'LL ALWAYS REMEMBER

The Editors

ONLY YESTERDAY

PEGGY WEBB

BANTAM BOOKS
NEW YORK · TORONTO · LONDON · SYDNEY · AUCKLAND

ONLY YESTERDAY
A Bantam Book / September 1998

LOVESWEPT *and the wave design are registered trademarks of Bantam Books, a division of Bantam Doubleday Dell Publishing Group, Inc. Registered in U.S. Patent and Trademark Office and elsewhere.*

All rights reserved.
Copyright © 1998 by Peggy Webb.
Cover art copyright © 1998 by Barney Plotkin.
No part of this book may be reproduced or transmitted in any form or by any means, electronic or mechanical, including photocopying, recording, or by any information storage and retrieval system, without permission in writing from the publisher.
For information address: Bantam Books.

If you purchased this book without a cover you should be aware that this book is stolen property. It was reported as "unsold and destroyed" to the publisher and neither the author nor the publisher has received any payment for this "stripped book."

ISBN 0-553-44633-9

Published simultaneously in the United States and Canada

Bantam Books are published by Bantam Books, a division of Bantam Doubleday Dell Publishing Group, Inc. Its trademark, consisting of the words "Bantam Books" and the portrayal of a rooster, is Registered in U.S. Patent and Trademark Office and in other countries. Marca Registrada. Bantam Books, 1540 Broadway, New York, New York 10036.

PRINTED IN THE UNITED STATES OF AMERICA

OPM   10 9 8 7 6 5 4 3 2 1

To Kate and David, Frank and Mo,
who offered me tea, sympathy,
and a spectacular view of
Penobscot Bay while I wrote this book;
and to Tom, always.

ONE

She hadn't set out to buy a clock that day. She'd been intent on getting a new latch for the screen door. But the temperature hovered near ninety, and Ann had detoured by the ice-cream shop to get something cool to eat, then she'd caught a glimpse of the sign over the door of the quaint little shop in the middle of the block. "Blast From The Past" the sign promised, and she wasn't disappointed by the delivery.

John Wayne, Marilyn Monroe, and James Dean stood in the back of the shop, life-size, cardboard smiles frozen for posterity. Through the speakers mounted over the soda fountain, Percy Sledge crooned, "When A Man Loves A Woman." A leather trunk plastered with stickers from the Hotel Palace in Mar del Plata and the Continental Hotel in Tangier hinted of grand adventures in times gone by.

But it was the clock that drew her to the shelves at

2

the back of the store, a black plastic cat, tail wagging, big pop eyes rolling.

"Aren't you the sassiest little thing?" Standing on tiptoe, she tried to get the clock off the shelf, but it was out of reach.

Out of the blue a pair of very tanned, very masculine hands plucked the clock from the shelf. Ann was not the kind of woman who agonized over possessions, but all of a sudden she wanted that clock in a way that made her almost frantic.

"That's my clock."

She whirled around, puffed up for a fight, but what she saw took the wind right out of her sails. He had a smile that would light the entire South in a blackout and enough body heat to raise the temperature ten degrees. He was standing so close, her nose was only inches away from his broad chest, and he showed no intention of moving. Furthermore, she'd stepped on his fine black leather boots.

"Pardon me." Her apology only increased his amusement. Ann wanted to hit something.

"Do you always talk to yourself?" he asked.

His voice matched the rest of him, big and dark and mysterious, the kind of voice that set foolish women shivering. Darned if she hadn't joined the ranks of the foolish. Her tank top was plastered to her back with sweat, but she was shivering like a willow in a spring storm. And over a perfect stranger.

Ann felt like a traitor. Unconsciously she twisted the diamond on her finger. The minute she got to Windchime House she would phone Rob.

Only Yesterday

3

"Don't you ever reply to anything anybody says to you?" She removed her foot from his boot and tried to take a step back, but the shelves were in her way. This gloriously gorgeous man had her trapped and had her clock, to boot, and she couldn't even muster up enough sparks for a singeing rebuke.

"Down here we do things in a more leisurely fashion."

Leaning in close, he propped one elbow on the shelf near her head. Ann wondered why swooning had gone out of style. For a moment she thought about reviving the lost Victorian art, right there in the heart of downtown Fairhope, Alabama.

"For instance, we introduce ourselves, and then if we like the person we've just met, we might sit down together and have a cool drink of lemonade." He turned up the voltage on his smile. "Colt Butler. I'm buying."

"I'm engaged."

The minute the words were out of her mouth she wanted to bite her tongue off. She sounded prissy and defensive, two qualities she deplored.

"My congratulations to the lucky man."

He actually tipped his hat, a battered old baseball cap without lettering, a faded butternut twill that looked soft to the touch. Ann curled her fingers tightly together to keep from reaching toward that tattered cap. Seeking relief, she slid her gaze lower. It came to rest on a pair of shocking blue eyes. As brilliant as neon. As mesmerizing as bits of bottle glass found in the surf.

When her toes curled under she knew she was in serious trouble. The Debeau curse.

"When your toes curl under, that's when you know," her aunt Gilly had told her. Had it been only three months ago?

"Know what, Aunt Gilly?"

"That it's true love."

Ann had laughed. She'd waited years for the famous Debeau sign, but when she'd met Rob she knew that love was choice, not fate. "Rob and I don't need silly signs. When something is right, it's right, Aunt Gilly."

"Sooner or later it happens to all the Debeau women."

"You're going to love Rob. You'll be the first to dance at our wedding. In fact, I'm going to send you a ticket so you can come up to New York and help me pick out the wedding dress."

A month later she'd sent the ticket, but by then it had been too late. Gilly Debeau was hospitalized, heavily sedated with painkillers, struggling through the final stages of the liver cancer nobody'd even known she had.

"Hey . . ." Colt Butler cupped her cheek, his hand warm and reassuring. "Are you all right? If it's the clock I—"

"It's not the clock." Ann tucked her dark hair behind her left ear, a habit Rob was trying to break her of.

Colt Butler took her arm, and before she could protest she was sitting beside him on a bar stool at the soda fountain.

"Two of your banana split specials, Marge," he said.

"That's very thoughtful of you." Ann didn't even tell him she'd just had a strawberry ice cream. What the heck? She'd skip supper. Not that there was anything in the cabinets to cook. She'd spent the days prior to Aunt Gilly's death at the hospital, and the days since the funeral organizing her aunt's possessions and trying to decide what to do about the house. Eating was secondary.

"How did you know I love ice cream?" She plowed into the banana split with gusto.

"I have this special radar. It hones in on fat gram counters a mile away. I always head in the opposite direction." Suddenly he leaned over and wiped the corner of her mouth with the tip of his index finger. Her toes curled under again.

"Berry juice," he said. "It looked so good, I started to lick it off."

"Shocking. And you don't even know my name."

Was that her laughing with such reckless abandon, as if she didn't have a care in the world, as if she didn't have the world's most wonderful man waiting for her in Brooklyn, as if Colt Butler didn't still have her Felix the Cat clock.

"What *is* your name?"

"Ann Debeau. Charlotte Ann, actually, named for my grandmother, only nobody ever calls me that except when I come back home to the South."

He studied her a long time, but never once during his intense scrutiny did she feel uncomfortable. And that surprised her almost as much as her toes curling under. She'd always guarded her privacy as much as she'd guarded her time. And yet here she was, telling this strange man things she'd never even told Rob.

"The name suits you." He nodded, adding his stamp of approval, then kissed her hand in the courtly manner of a long-ago era. "I'm pleased to meet you, Annie Debeau."

Annie. Something stirred inside her, as soft as the brush of angel wings. Nobody had ever called her Annie, and yet the name felt as familiar to her as if she awakened every day to the sound of it on her lover's lips.

"I might reciprocate except that you stole my clock right out from under my nose."

"This sassy little thing?" The clock's tail never missed a beat as Colt set it on the counter.

"You were eavesdropping."

"No. I was right behind you, thinking the same thing myself. Only not about the clock."

With any other man she would have taken offense, but Colt had a warm, easy manner that allowed him to pass off outrageous remarks as refreshing honesty.

"You probably say that to all the girls."

"Probably," he agreed, laughing to himself.

Later she would mull over the encounter bit by bit, as she always did, and be mortified at her own behavior, but the heat and the banana split, combined with Colt Butler's natural charm, put her in a mellow mood. He could suggest they swim naked in the moonlight, and she doubted she'd blink twice.

"So you're at Windchime House?" he added.

Only Yesterday

"How did you know?"

"The name. Your grandmother's house is a familiar landmark around here. Beautiful and strangely haunting in a way I can't describe."

"Exactly." She was amazed that he'd seen beyond the beauty.

"Do you ever swim naked in the bay?"

She nearly dropped her spoon. "In the moonlight?"

"Yes." It was his turn to be flustered.

"Do you read minds?" she asked.

"No. I barely have time to read newspapers." Under the guise of savoring his cherries and whipped cream, he studied her. "You were thinking the same thing?"

"I don't want you to get the wrong idea."

"Neither do I. I've been called a rake and a Southern-fried Romeo, but I've never been called a cad." He lifted her hand and twisted the ring on her finger. "The first thing you told me was that you'd made a pledge, and I respect that." His grin was wicked. "I don't like it, but I respect it."

Why was it, the simplest little thing he said could make her hot all over? What she needed was a good dose of Rob. His practical manner was the perfect counterbalance for her unconventional, unpredictable nature, the perfect antidote for the outrageous man sitting beside her.

"Thanks for the ice cream, Colt. I have to run, I have a million things to do."

"You didn't finish."

She gazed with longing at her dish. Laughing, Colt

scooped up the whipped cream and cherries, and held the spoon to her mouth. How could she resist?

"You always save the best for last," he said.

"How did you know?" He offered another bite, and she took it.

"I do too." He scraped the last bite from her bowl, then cupped her chin while she ate.

She closed her eyes in sheer appreciation of the moment—the ice cream, the ceiling fans stirring the balmy air, the tender touch of a man's hand on her skin.

"Hmmm . . . the last bite *is* always the best."

Suddenly she felt another touch, on her lips this time, whisper-soft, gentle as dew falling on roses. Colt's lips on hers.

It was a brief kiss, so brief that when she opened her eyes she thought she might have dreamed it. Except for the gleam in his eyes.

"So it is," he murmured.

She jumped off the stool. "I have to be going."

"I know. You have a million things to do."

His smile caught her hard up under her rib cage, and for a moment she thought she might faint. Unable to take her eyes off him, she angled sideways toward the door muttering, "Pardon me," more times than she could count as she bumped into hapless bystanders and stepped on toes.

She was as confused as Alice in Wonderland. Swinging open the door, she gulped deep breaths of fresh air.

"You forgot something."

His voice was all too familiar. Familiar, too, was the floating sensation she felt from something as simple as the sound of his voice.

"You forgot this."

There was the clock in all its forties splendor, tail merrily wagging, eyes rolling as if Felix the Cat knew things nobody else knew.

"But I didn't forget it. It's yours. You got to it first."

"No. You were there first." He pressed the clock into her hands. "I want to buy it for you."

"Here." She reached into her purse. "How much—?"

He stilled her with a firm grip over her hand. "My gift to you, Annie Debeau. To mark the time until we meet again."

Before she could protest he strolled over to the cashier, turning only long enough for a wink and a smile.

Felix the Cat sat on the mantel, looking as out of place in Windchime House as a thorn on a morning glory.

"Rob?" Curled into a ball on the Victorian love seat, Ann cradled the receiver close.

"Honey?" The static on the line made him sound as if he were on another planet. And that's exactly how Ann felt, as if Rob were on Jupiter and she'd been abandoned somewhere between the moon and Venus. "What's wrong?"

"Does something have to be wrong for me to call you?"

"No. But we usually call each other in the evening, so the question stands."

"Nothing." Certainly nothing she could tell him.

"Is there something on your mind, Ann?"

Where was that rush of relief she'd expected to feel when she called him? Where was the lifting of the spirits, the music in the heart?

It had been too long since she'd seen him: That was all.

"Rob, did I ever tell you I was born the day my grandmother died?"

"No."

"You don't sound very interested."

"Now, Ann, don't get your dander up. I know it's been rough down there these last few weeks, but, honey, it's the middle of the afternoon."

Why was it that everything he said irritated her?

"Well, don't let me keep you from your clients."

"I am on a tight schedule today—contracts to get out, Charlie Battingham breathing down my neck, getting ready for court tomorrow, plus the usual mountain of paper on my desk. It's hell around here."

"It's pretty hot down here too."

Rob didn't even chuckle. "I'll call you tonight, honey, after you're all tucked in bed."

"Okay. Fine."

She held on to the receiver, waiting for him to say something more. Maybe she was expecting too much. Maybe dealing with her aunt's death had made her want more from life. But shouldn't there be words of comfort and tenderness and longing? Shouldn't there be soft sighs and heavy breathing? Shouldn't there be a mention of love?

"Is there something else, Ann?"

"No. Nothing. 'Bye, Rob."

"Good-bye, Ann. Talk to you later."

She hugged her legs and pressed her cheek on her knees, taking comfort from the sweaty feel of her own skin and the smell of the lotion she'd found in Aunt Gilly's bathroom. Rose. A favorite scent of the Debeau women. It was everywhere—in the potpourri on the marble-topped tables, in the drying petals of the huge bouquets friends had sent for the memorial services. The sweet scent even clung to the velvet drapes, as if cascades of rose petals had been crushed against the heavy fabric.

Suddenly Ann couldn't breathe. Barefoot, she padded onto the front porch. It was more properly called a veranda, spanning the entire front of the white three-story house that overlooked the water and wrapping halfway around the sides. The sun streaked the western sky with magenta and purple, and ceiling fans stirred the humid air, setting the wind chimes asway. First her grandmother and then her aunt had collected them from all over the world, tuned chimes whose tinkling music carried across the wide sweep of lawn and down to the dock where a sailboat lay at anchor.

Ann leaned on the front porch rail and looked out across the water. The bay was spectacular in the setting sun, a scene that was balm to an artist's soul.

She could work here. For the hundredth time in the last few days she wondered what she was going to do about Windchime House. It had belonged to her grandmother, then her aunt Gilly, and now it was hers.

But her life was in New York. Wasn't it?

The sea lapped against the shore, its music as compelling as a siren's song. Ann looked out over the water and thought about swimming naked in the moonlight.

TWO

Colt's mind wasn't on the movie, and it certainly wasn't on the woman at his side—Linda Levine, the new pharmacist at Harco. He'd been looking forward to their date all week, but now he could barely suppress a yawn as they sat in the darkened theater. He wished he were home with his Labs.

"Do you want to stay for the rest of the movie?" he asked.

"Whatever you want."

An early night was what he wanted, an hour in his easy chair with a good Whitley Strieber book, Buck and Sam curled at his feet, then that long, deep fall into a dreamless sleep. But he owed Linda more than a quick dismissal.

"How about ice cream?"

"Great."

He took her to Blast From The Past, hoping to rid himself of the spell he'd been under since early afternoon. But the minute he walked in the door the memories came flooding back—the shapely tanned legs, the tiny nipped-in waist, the shining cap of black hair that slid across one cheek when she tilted her head, the incredible green eyes.

But more than the memory was the feeling, as if he'd been squeezed high up under the ribs, as if he'd come face-to-face with one of his own dreams.

"What a glorious place," Linda said. "Do you come here often?"

"It's a favorite haunt of mine." The same bar stools he and Annie had sat on were empty, but Colt steered Linda in the opposite direction. "What kind of ice cream do you like?"

"Sorbet or sherbet." She laughed at the expression on his face. "Too many fat grams in the real stuff."

An hour later Colt was in his own den, both dogs rubbing against his legs, vying for his attention.

"I had a narrow escape, boys, from a fat gram counter. Man, I can't believe I made such a mistake."

"Talking to the dogs again?"

Colt's spirits lifted every time he saw his uncle Pete. Grizzled and bowlegged, with more hair in his eyebrows than on his head, he was still the grandest man Colt had ever known, mother and father to him since Colt was five years old, the best parent in Alabama, the best horse trainer in the world.

"Who is there to talk to except you, and all you want to talk about is horses?"

Pete chuckled. "Let's talk about women then."

"You don't know squat about women."

"Neither do you, from all I can hear."

"You shouldn't listen to idle gossip."

"It wasn't idle; it was solicited."

Laughing, Colt slung his arm around his uncle's shoulders, towering over the old man. "What am I going to do with you, you old reprobate?"

"Marry and give me grandchildren."

"What? And make Buck and Sam jealous? Not a chance."

Colt had given more than a passing thought to Uncle Pete's proposal, but somehow he managed to find fault with every woman he dated. And their numbers were legion.

He and his uncle shared a glass of iced tea in the kitchen before Pete climbed the stairs to go to bed.

Colt had intended to do the same thing himself. Tomorrow would be a long day. Starfire was being delivered from Kentucky, and he and Pete would need all their resources to settle the Thoroughbred into his new home.

But something else claimed Colt's attention, drawing him out the back door and past the paddocks to an ancient stone barn partially covered with ivy. The barn had been built in 1870 and was one of the original structures on Colt's estate in Point Clear. He'd converted it to an office, mainly for the view of the rolling polo fields beyond the window, but also because of its architectural features.

It was cool inside, a tribute to the builders who

knew the value of thick stone walls in the Southern heat. Ancient beams crisscrossed the vaulted ceiling, and thick cypress shelves suspended high above the work area displayed Colt's collection of pottery. He turned on the floodlights. Flowerpots and teapots and bowls and urns came into view, handmade pottery of all sizes and shapes.

Colt rolled the ladder to a stop before an intricately designed urn, one that looked as if it had been done by ancient Egyptians. Carefully he lifted it down, then set it on his desk and traced the potter's name, carved in the bottom.

He'd stumbled onto the small gallery in Soho five years earlier, and had fallen in love with the piece in his hand. "A brilliant young artist," the proprietor had told him. "Up and coming. Soon everybody will be clamoring for a piece of work by Ann Debeau."

Though Colt had a knack for acquiring horses that the polo world would soon be clamoring for, he didn't purchase art for the same reason. He didn't care if the work would increase in value. It didn't matter to him whether the artist was well known or would never be heard of. He bought for one reason only: The work had to speak to his soul.

More than any other piece of pottery on his shelves, Annie's urn spoke to his soul. Not only his soul, but also his heart. High on the shelves underneath the lights it was a beautiful work worthy of admiration, but in his hands it was alive, as if the heart of the artist pulsed there as well.

Tracing the intricate design, he pictured Annie—

dynamic, vibrant, a tiny china doll. She was not at all what he would have expected, and yet she was absolutely perfect.

He caressed the work of art she'd created, and his palms grew hot. The air around him became charged with energy. It was the same electricity he'd felt earlier that afternoon in the little shop downtown when he'd kissed Annie.

A strange impulse, that kiss. Almost as if magnets were pulling him toward her lush lips.

Colt turned off the lights and went back to the house. Sprawled in the middle of a bed handmade from lightning-struck cedars that hadn't survived the storm of '36, he dreamed of swimming naked in the moonlight with Annie, her hair grown long and floating behind them like a banner of ebony silk.

THREE

"Flowers for Miss Ann Debeau." The delivery boy held a huge bouquet of orchids. Ann tipped him generously, then ripped open the card.

"Only one more day. Can't wait to see you, Rob."

Ann parted her way through boxes and set the bouquet on a Victorian table beside the French doors. Margaret Finley left the box she was packing to admire the beautiful blooms.

"Nice. They must be from that young man Gilly told me about."

In Brooklyn such a personal remark would have been considered intrusive, but Margaret Finley had been Gilly Debeau's friend since the two of them were in first grade. There was nothing Gilly didn't tell her. She was almost like family.

"He wants me to come home," Ann said.

"You don't sound too excited about it."

"It's not that I don't want to see Rob. There's just

so much to do here. I don't know whether to store the furniture or let it stay here. I don't know whether to sell the house or keep it."

"You know what I always told Gilly? Don't let outside pressures color your decisions." She put her arm around Ann's shoulders. "Honey, you've got to make up your own mind in your own time. That young fellow in New York will wait."

"Thanks, Margaret. I don't know what I would have done these last few weeks without you."

"If something's going on, I'm right in the middle of it. Gilly says . . ." Quick tears sprang to her eyes. "Lordy, what am I going to do without her?"

"You have me." Both of them were thinking that soon Ann would be in New York, but neither of them mentioned it. "Here, let's get these things into your car."

"You shouldn't be giving me all these clothes and jewelry."

"Aunt Gilly would want you to have them."

By the time Margaret drove off, dusk was falling. Ann went inside, kicked off her shoes, and turned on the lamps. She was in the kitchen making a tuna sandwich when the doorbell rang.

Margaret must have forgotten something. Ann didn't even put on her shoes.

"Margaret?" she called as she padded to the door.

"Sorry to disappoint you."

He was taller than she remembered, more vibrant somehow, as if standing on the front porch of

Windchime House had added to his considerable appeal.

"Oh, my." Ann's heart fluttered like hummingbird wings. She put her hand over her chest in hopes of slowing it down.

"I could say I was just passing by and decided to drop in, but the fact is I was out riding today and saw a bank of flowers that reminded me of you, and so I dismounted and separated them from the thorny bush at great peril to myself."

From behind his back Colt Butler produced a huge bouquet of the most beautiful wild pink roses Ann had ever seen. She was extraordinarily pleased, then immediately felt guilty. She couldn't continue taking gifts and flowers from this man.

"Consider them a belated memorial to your aunt," he said, as if he'd read her mind.

"My favorite. Color and all." She buried her face in the fragrant petals. "How did you know?"

"Logical. They match your skin."

"Thank you for the flowers."

"I was hoping you'd invite me in so I could see the inside of this house."

"Of course. Come in."

She stepped aside for him to pass, but when he saw her bare feet he stopped squarely in front of her.

"Hmm, nice." The way he looked at her made her sizzle. "Nothing is sexier than a pretty woman in bare feet."

"I'll get my shoes."

He followed her into the kitchen. "Afterward, I can show you how to turn that tuna into a gourmet meal."

"Afterward?" Shoes forgotten, she felt herself blushing.

His chuckle was wicked. "After the tour."

In addition to being flustered, she felt slightly treacherous. Why did Colt's wild roses please her more than Rob's hothouse orchids? And why was she more excited over the prospect of showing Windchime House to this gorgeous interloper than at the prospect of going home to her fiancé?

What she would do is get the tour over as quickly as possible, then sit down to her tuna all by herself, and concentrate on the things she should be thinking about—the house, Rob, the wedding . . . Good grief. She was getting married in six months.

"We'll make this a quick tour," she said, but she was soon caught up in his enthusiasm.

Hearing his extravagant praise, she felt almost as if she were seeing Windchime House for the first time. Family portraits lined the wall as they climbed the stairs, and he lingered in front of each one, asking dozens of questions.

"My father, James . . . a doctor . . . died in a plane crash, six years ago . . . My mother, Lisa . . . she lives in Paris. Those two were painted by Fiorella Sabatini."

"These two are painted by a different artist." It was not a question. Colt had a good eye.

"Yes. The artist is Porter Rockland. Aunt Gilly at sixteen, and my grandfather Richard Debeau, painted the day my father was born. That's the reason he looks so harried. He'd scheduled the sitting months prior to the date, never guessing that Daddy would make his entrance two months early. Poor Grandpa. They say he raced back and forth between the bedroom and the sunroom so many times, he wore a path in the carpet."

Ann didn't know why laughter came so freely with this man. Nor could she say why she felt such ease in his company, ease with an underlying current that she dared not name.

The portrait at the top of the stairs mesmerized Colt. "This is you?"

"No. My grandmother, painted when she was eighteen."

"Incredible." He alternately studied the portrait, then Ann. "I would have sworn it was you dressed for some kind of costume ball. You're a dead ringer."

Ann never looked at the portrait without the eerie feeling that she was looking inside herself. Charlotte Ann Harris Debeau had the dewy look of a woman in love. Her eyes were shining, her lips were slightly parted as if she'd been surprised by a kiss, and her skin had the natural flush of a woman who had just been thoroughly loved.

The woman in the portrait seemed to beckon them closer. They studied her, standing side by side, so close, their thighs were touching. Even that small contact gave Ann goose bumps. She knew she should move away, but her feet seemed to be glued to the floor.

"That's amazing work," Colt said. "Such power, such passion. Who is the artist?"

Only Yesterday

23

"Anthony Chance. His body of work was small, but it's considered the best portrait art of the twentieth century."

"His use of color and shading rivals the masters."

"You know art."

"Pottery, mostly." Colt took her hands, studied her palms, traced her fingers, then bent down and placed a gentle kiss in each palm.

"Thank you, Ann Debeau, for hours of pleasure." She sucked in a sharp breath, and his eyes twinkled. "I have one of your pieces. It's the prize of my collection."

"In view of such high praise, how can I refuse to share my humble tuna with you."

Colt was enchanted. That was the only reason he could think of for staying at Windchime House until almost eleven o'clock. The house had cast a spell.

Or was it the woman? She was a soft woman, given to quick laughter and feminine gestures that melted him right down to the tips of his well-worn leather boots.

Did she feel the magic, too, or was she truly in love with the man who waited for her in New York? It wouldn't do to pursue that line of thought.

The clock in the hallway chimed the half hour. She followed him to the front porch, still barefoot.

The wind whipped her hair into her face, and she tucked it behind one ear. He pictured her on the beach wearing a white dress that flowed around her, tucking her hair behind her ear. The image was so real, he passed his hands over his eyes to clear his vision.

Drops of rain as big as dinner plates splatted onto the front porch.

"There's a storm brewing. You be careful, Annie."

"I'll be gone long before the storm. I leave early in the morning."

Something lurched inside him, as powerful as a ship torn loose from its moorings.

"Can I drive you to the airport?"

"I have the rental car. But thanks anyway." She held out her hand, as tiny and delicate as a flower. "And thank you for the roses."

He solemnly shook her hand, then pressed another quick, hot kiss in her palm, a heroic gesture considering what he wanted to do.

"Your life should be filled with roses, Annie Debeau."

She stood on the porch, waving until he was out of sight, the wind whipping her hair, her bare toes curled under.

It was an image that stayed with him on the drive down scenic 98, round the bend past the Grand Hotel, and beyond the Point Clear Polo Club to the gentle slopes and curving paths of his own estate.

The image was still with him the next day when the storm off the coast of Florida built force, veered westward, and was dubbed Hurricane Bethany. He was in the stables checking on a new foal when the call came to evacuate.

There would be no evacuation for Colt. He would stay with his horses.

"I'll round up the horses in the west pasture and secure the ones in the lower meadow," he told Pete.

Further inland than Windchime House, he was not in the same danger as the residents along the shore. His slicker was scant protection from the storm. Wind was gusting so high that young trees were bent double, and torrential rains quickly turned small streams on his property to swiftly moving, treacherous creeks.

The high-strung polo ponies shied away every time a tree limb popped, bucking and rearing against the howling winds that whipped their tails and manes and the blinding rains that blotted out the landscape.

Colt leaned low over his mount, Warrior, a tried-and-true stallion who had served his time on the fields and was now retired to bask in the sunshine, roll in the meadows, and carry his master on an occasional leisurely jaunt around the estate.

"Steady there, now." Colt rubbed Warrior's neck. "Bring them in, boy."

He squinted, trying to see the barn. Failing that, he relied on his instinct to take him and his valuable horses in the right direction. As the horses thundered ahead of him, Colt said a prayer of thanksgiving that Annie was safe in New York.

FOUR

"I just heard the news, Ann. What's going on down there?" The phone lines crackled, and Ann pressed the receiver closer to her ear.

"It's a hurricane, Rob."

"Good Lord. I told you not to change your plane reservations."

Ann gripped the receiver so hard, her knuckles turned white. Lately she seemed always to be defending herself to Rob. "There's still a lot I have to do before I can come home."

"The newscaster said they were evacuating Fairhope."

"I know that. You don't have to make it sound like an accusation."

"I'm scared for you, Ann. That's all."

She sighed. "I know. I'm sorry. I've been on edge ever since Aunt Gilly got sick." A tree branch tore loose from a large magnolia and crashed onto the front porch. She jumped, and the receiver clattered to the floor.

"Ann? *Ann?*"

"I'm here. I just dropped the phone."

"You've got to get out of there, Ann. Do you still have the car?"

"Yes." She looked out the window, searching for the rental car, a small red sedan, but all she saw was a solid wall of gray rain.

"Then leave. Now. Call me as soon as you get out."

"It'll be hours, Rob. The only way out is across the Causeway, and the latest report is that traffic is backed up all the way to Daphne."

"Just go. Call me."

"Okay." She had her lips all pursed to say, "I love you," but he'd already hung up.

Ann raced upstairs for her shoes and her raincoat, threw her toiletries into a small flight bag, then hurried downstairs. The wind tore the front door from her hands and it slammed against the wall so hard, the panes rattled. Bending her head against the wind and rain, Ann fought her way to the car. By the time she got behind the wheel, she was soaked through to the skin.

She inched down the driveway, the road barely visible. There were no other vehicles on scenic 98, and she was buoyed by her progress.

"At this rate I'll be across the Causeway before dark."

The sound of her own voice comforted her. She had grown up in Fairhope, but she had been too young to remember the only hurricane that had actually hit that part of the coast. All she remembered were the tales her parents and Aunt Gilly had told about Hurricane Dianne.

"Some fools had hurricane parties and died on their own rooftops," her daddy had said.

"A whole pig floated through the lobby of the Grand Hotel" was Aunt Gilly's favorite story.

Ann's tires parted the water already rising over the highway, and it spewed out behind her like the wake of a rowboat. The small curving hill onto Fairhope Avenue had disappeared in the gray rain, and she breathed a sigh of relief when she finally reached the bottom. But her relief was short-lived. Traffic was backed up all the way to Summit Street, bumper to bumper, inching along at a snail's pace.

Ann kept the car radio on.

"Evacuate now," the announcer said. "Fairhope will be in the eye of Hurricane Bethany."

He called out a number of statistics, all of them grim and frightening—wave crests and flood levels and wind velocity. Ann tried to sing to cheer herself up, but she petered out on the second verse of "Love Lifted Me."

Strange that she had chosen a hymn as emotional shelter from the storm. It led her to thinking about her argument with Rob over whether to have the wedding ceremony in the church or in his parents' home on Long Island.

"It'll be so much nicer at home," he'd said. "Then

we can step right outside to the pool for the reception."

"Vows exchanged in front of a fireplace don't have the same appeal as vows exchanged in front of an altar," she'd said, but like most of her arguments with Rob, she was losing this one.

Her car rocked and swayed in the deepening waters, and the clock on the dashboard told her that it had taken two hours to go four blocks. People began abandoning their cars, some striking out toward the highway, others turning back to their homes.

"Accidents are piling up on the Causeway. It's totally blocked," the announcer said. "Do not attempt to cross. Repeat. Do not attempt to cross."

Ann's heart sank. It was too late. There was no way she could evacuate.

She tried to steer the little car off the road, but the waters caught her and swept her sideways, almost through the window of Fairhope Pharmacy. It took all her strength to shove her door open against the force of the rising water, then she bent her head and started in the direction she hoped was home.

An expert pilot, Colt was one of the first people to volunteer for rescue operations. His office in the barn housed his emergency communications system as well as a generator-operated refrigerator and hot plate, a well-stocked pantry and cots for him and Uncle Pete.

Exhausted from long hours herding horses into the

barn, Pete was snoring on the cot while Colt listened through his headphones.

"It's going to be bad," Wayne Dozzier said. He was chief of the Fairhope Fire Department as well as a Vietnam vet and helicopter pilot.

"How bad?"

"Best I can tell, at least half the folks between Ingleside Street and Mobile Bay got trapped."

"Windchime House?" He didn't know what made him ask the question. By now Annie was in New York and in the arms of another man.

"Best we can tell, that house is vacant."

Colt should have felt relief. Instead he felt as if a ghost had walked on his grave.

"I'll start working the area along scenic Route 98 as soon as I can."

"Don't do any heroic stuff, Colt. Wait till I give you the all-clear signal."

"You got it, pal."

Colt tumbled into his cot but his sleep was troubled by visions of Annie standing at a window calling his name.

Ann knew the waters would rise. She'd lost track of time since she bailed out of her car and half-walked, half-floated back to Windchime House. She'd immediately packed rations and emergency supplies, and stowed them in the attic, and now she struggled with the family portraits.

Her grandmother's portrait was the first up the

stairs. "I won't let the waters destroy you," she promised her ancestor. Her only answer was the winds howling around the eaves of her house.

Strange how the disaster had changed her thinking about Windchime House. The day before she'd been trying to decide whether to sell the house, and now she was thinking of it as her own.

It was midnight by the time Ann got all the portraits to the attic. She was making herself a pallet beside an old trunk when another thought struck her.

She raced downstairs and rescued the bouquet of roses Colt had brought to her. On the way to the staircase she passed the hall table where Rob's orchids sat.

"I'll have to come back for you. My hands are full."

Suddenly all the lights went out, and she stumbled up the stairs in the dark. While she'd been gone, the winds had ripped open the attic window, and the force of the winds knocked her off her feet. She fumbled for her flashlight, then struggled to get the windows closed and bolted.

Exhausted, she fell onto her pallet, and awakened shivering an hour later. The house was shivering, too, pitching and groaning in the hurricane that lashed the coast of south Alabama.

"I didn't bring enough covers. Isn't that just like an absentminded artist?"

Trying to keep her spirits up, Ann kept talking to herself as she turned on her flashlight and lifted the lid of the trunk.

"Everybody keeps quilts in a trunk, don't they . . . ? Eureka!"

There it was, right on top, a beautiful coverlet made of velvet and satin and yellowing lace, each patch painstakingly stitched with exquisite satin embroidery. Ann lifted out the quilt, intent on covering herself and going back to sleep, then her eyes fell on the packet of letters.

The letter on top was addressed to "Miss Charlotte Ann Harris" and postmarked "October 7, 1942." Intrigued, Ann riffled through the stack. They were all addressed to her grandmother, all dated from World War II.

Outside the wind roared like a freight train, snapping trees as if they were twigs and slamming them into Windchime House. Holding the letters in a death grip, Ann wrapped her arms around herself, shivering.

She was stranded, alone in the hurricane. But she wasn't going to let herself dwell on all the horrible possibilities. Bundled up in the quilt, she sat on her pallet and opened the first of her grandmother's letters.

FIVE

"Dearest Annie . . ."

Her grandfather had never called her grandmother anything except Charlotte Ann. Or so she'd been told. Ann knew nothing of his years in the war, either. She read on, eager to learn more about the ancestor whose name she bore.

"I'm sitting on the deck of the U.S.S. *Montpelier*, which will be my home for the next several months. There's a beautiful phosphorescence to the waters that makes it easier for the Japanese to spot our ship, but all I can think about is you, about the way you looked in the moonlight, your hair hanging down your back like a bolt of silk, your white dress blowing in the wind. I still taste your lips, my love. I still feel your soft skin against mine. I still smell the roses in your hair."

Ann blinked away sudden tears. The letter in her hand was one of the most romantic things she'd ever read. It thrilled her that her grandparents had had such a passionate relationship. She'd never known her grandmother, but judging by Richard Debeau's stern demeanor, she would never have guessed him capable of such deep feelings, let alone such romantic prose.

She read on: "In the wild, dark beauty of the night with the crescent moon and the stars overhead, a million twinkling lights, you'd never guess at the ugliness of Tulagi. Shells have gutted the island, uprooted trees, and gouged huge holes which are filled with the awful remains of the dead. I carry your picture next to my heart, always, so that I have beauty at my fingertips, beauty of mind, body, and spirit, beauty of heart, beauty of soul."

Rob had never said such lovely things to her.

"Silly goose," she chided herself. He was an industrious, practical man, totally committed to her. What more did she want? Ann turned to the second page of the love letter to her grandmother.

"I love you deeply, madly, my darling Annie. I love you with the deepest yearnings of my being, and I will love you till the day I die. Yours forever, Anthony."

Anthony? Ann folded the letter, stuffed it back and studied the front of the envelope, searching for the truth. There it was in fine artistic script in the upper left-hand corner of the envelope, right over "The U.S.S. *Montpelier.*" *A. Chance.*

Her grandmother's lover was none other than the artist who had painted her portrait: Anthony Chance.

That explained the flushed, dewy look the artist had captured. Anthony Chance had painted a woman in love.

Only Yesterday

35

Who was this man her grandmother had loved, and what had happened to him, to them? Why had Charlotte Ann Harris married Richard Debeau instead of Anthony Chance?

Ann opened the second letter, and a photograph slid to the floor. She felt around in the dark, then trained her flashlight around the area. There on the dusty attic floor was a small black-and-white snapshot, a young pilot standing beside his plane.

Ann bent closer, and suddenly she stopped breathing. Smiling back at her from the ancient photograph was a face she knew, the chiseled cheekbones, the square chin, the dark, untamed hair, the sensuous lips curved into a smile that made her heart ache. Anthony Chance smiled back at her with Colt Butler's face.

She expelled a slow breath as she traced the outline of the man in the yellowed photograph. It was all there, the tall frame, the wide shoulders, the large, capable hands. Even the way he stood, legs slightly apart, feet firmly planted as if he'd just laid claim to the patch of earth he stood on.

It was exactly the way Colt Butler had stood on the front porch of Windchime House. What was it he had said about the house? "It's beautiful and strangely haunting . . ."

Hands trembling, she began to read: "My darling Annie, In a few hours I'll take the Black Cat up for night maneuvers over the Solomons. The takeoff from the deck of the *Montpelier* will be a piece of cake, but landings are always tricky, particularly night landings.

"Best not to dwell on it. Pilots who do tend to

freeze up. While I'm flying over the Pacific I'll think about you, my dearest love. I'll remember the last evening we had together before I left . . . the waters of the bay shot through with moonlight, your skin flashing silver as you swam toward me, the way you rose up naked from the sea, a passionate mermaid, a gift from the gods. I can still feel the waters lapping at us as we came together, and the sand that coated us when I carried you to the beach and lay with you there."

"Do you ever swim naked in the bay?" Colt had said.
"In the moonlight?" she'd replied.

Ann could feel the water against her bare skin, could see the shining pathway the moonlight made across the bay, could see the smiling face of the man who held out his arms as she began to swim. Anthony Chance. Colt Butler.

A large weight sat on her chest, and she stood up to keep from smothering. A flash from the troubled heavens briefly illuminated the ancient steamer trunk, the packet of letters, the single snapshot on the dusty attic floor.

She was not the one who had swum in the bay. Her grandmother had been. And not with Colt Butler, but with Anthony Chance.

The letter hadn't named the bay. Perhaps it wasn't even Mobile Bay. She was reading a love story from another time, another place.

To keep her mind off the mayhem outside, to keep from thinking that she might die alone in the attic, Ann picked up the packet of letters and continued to read.

Only Yesterday

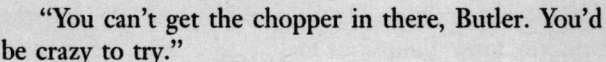

"You can't get the chopper in there, Butler. You'd be crazy to try."

"Then call me crazy."

"Butler, wait . . ."

Colt didn't wait to hear what Wayne Dozzier said. All he could think about was the floodwaters that engulfed two floors of Windchime House, and the distress signal, a white sheet that flapped from the attic window. All he could think about was the woman trapped inside.

Annie. He had to get to Annie.

The chopper lifted, and he was on his way. Below him a tight knot of rescue workers watched from the slick tarmac, fatigue written in every line of their faces and bodies. They'd been working for two days and nights without rest, basing their rescue operations from Pensacola. Dozens of people had been placed in temporary shelter, awaiting the time when they could return to flood-ravaged homes and begin the long, slow process of making them habitable once more.

But there were still people trapped, among them, Annie. From the moment Wayne had reported seeing the white sheet flying from her window, Colt had been a man obsessed. Nothing could stop him from going to her, neither floodwaters nor crosswinds nor exposed power lines.

He could see her rooftop now, a tiny dark blot in the distance. Flying closer, he saw the tops of the huge magnolia trees that had stood sentinel on the lawn for hundreds of years, saw the flag of white blowing in the winds that gusted over the bay. His helicopter bucked like a wild stallion. He banked left and scanned the window for a glimpse of life.

There. At the window. A shadow.

"Annie! ANNIE!"

The chopper shuddered and threatened to plunge. Colt fought for control, wrestling the heavy machine back into the sky. The sheet receded until it was merely a white dot.

"Dammit, I'm not going to give up."

His teeth clenched, the skin at his jaw pulled so tight, his face hurt, Colt went in for another attempt at rescue. This time Annie saw him. She stood at the window, waving frantically.

"I'm coming, Annie. I'm coming."

He eased the big bird lower, talking it down. "Come on, baby. You can do it now. Come on. I'm counting on you."

Annie was leaning out the window, screaming something, but the wind caught her voice and carried it away.

"Hang on, Annie," he yelled, knowing she couldn't hear.

The roof grew bigger and bigger.

"I'm going to make it this time. I've got to make it."

He could feel the power of the winds against his frail aircraft. He could feel the rage of the hurricane's aftermath. Suddenly he was snatched up and tossed about like a sponge football. Treetops came toward him at a dizzying speed.

Colt wrestled for control. "You're not going to do this to me," he shouted. "You're not going to claim another victim," he yelled. "Not yet. Not till I get Annie."

But he knew that it was useless to try once more to reach her by helicopter. Unless he wanted to die. And dying was the last thing on his mind.

Finally he got the bird under control. "I'll be back for you," he yelled, then set an easterly course toward Pensacola.

Ann watched the helicopter disappear into a sky the color of old pewter.

"I'm not going to cry," she said, but she did anyhow, huge tears that scalded her cheeks and clogged her throat.

"What am I going to do now?"

Fatigue overcame her as she slumped against the dusty floor, and she dozed. When she woke up she was ravenous, and she opened a tin of Vienna sausage, plucked out two fat sticks, and ate them along with three saltines.

"A meal fit for a king." She set the rest of the sausages aside. She didn't know how long she would be trapped in the attic, and she had no intention of starving to death because she didn't have the discipline to ration her meager stockpile of food.

From a dusty corner, Felix the Cat winked at her. All of a sudden she felt better.

"Who are you flirting with, you sassy thing? I must look like something the cats dragged up and the dogs wouldn't have. Pardon my expression."

What to do now? She went to the attic window and surveyed her situation. Water as far as she could see. Even if she tried to swim to safety, where would she go?

She'd done all she could. The bedsheet, her distress signal, flapped in the wind. She checked to see if it was securely fastened, then cracked the attic door to check the level of floodwater. It lapped at the third step below the attic.

All she could do was wait and hope the floodwaters didn't rise any farther. She settled onto her pallet, picked up the packet of letters, and continued to read: "My darling, Not much sleep, not much time. Heavy bombing all around. Landed my torpedo bomber-fighter last night with the landing gear shot away. Thought my goose was cooked. Almost ran out of fuel circling. The two crewmen kept praying, and all I could think about was you. 'Can't let Annie down. I promised to return for her.' The red running lights on the *Montpelier*'s masthead looked like Christmas candles. 'Get the milk and cookies ready,' I yelled, ' 'Cause here comes Santa Claus.' I wish you could have heard the cheer that went up when I got that TBF back onto the carrier.

"And now I'm saying the same thing to you, my darling. 'Get the milk and cookies ready, 'cause here comes Santa Claus.' I'm coming back to you, Annie. I will return for you, my love. Always."

Dusk began to claim the landscape, and Ann lit a candle and set it in the window.

"Just in case," she whispered. "Just in case."

SIX

Soon it would be dark and Colt wouldn't be able to see the treacherous currents that threatened to catch his boat and hurl it into oblivion. He thrust the throttle forward, and the boat bucked like an ornery stallion before it plunged ahead at a speed he knew was foolhardy under the circumstances. Power lines down and floating God-only-knew where, swift currents churned up by Hurricane Bethany waiting to suck him under.

"Wait until conditions are better," Wayne had said to him. "Wait until the waters begin to recede and you can see what you're doing."

"Wait and let her die up there? Is that what you're saying?"

"Ann Debeau was at the window. You said so yourself."

"Can you predict whether the waters will rise or recede, Wayne?"

"Wish I could." Wayne knew he was engaged in a

losing battle. He put a hand on Colt's shoulder. "Be careful. There are hundreds of people who still need you."

Colt knew that, but right now his focus was on only one, the woman trapped in Windchime House.

He peered through the gray mists and the thickening darkness, wondering if he'd steered off course. Suddenly, out of the gloom he saw it, the tops of massive magnolias and ancient oaks, the gabled roof and bookend chimneys of Windchime House. And in the attic window he saw the light.

Colt gave a whoop of joy, throttled back, and steered his small craft through the swirling waters. Focused on the light in the window, he almost didn't see it, the power line that coiled like a snake in his path.

He swerved, barely missing it. But that was not the last of the obstacles. Trees floated in his path, parts of dismembered cars, entire rooftops.

The venerable magnolia that stood in the front yard of Windchime House was just up ahead, its top standing above the floodwaters like a giant green flag. If he could only make it to the tree, he'd have a chance.

He focused all his energy on the tree.

The sound woke her. A roaring sound, like a small plane. Disoriented, Ann sat up, the letters scattering about her.

He had come back. Just as he'd promised.

"Anthony?"

She stumbled across the floor, the candle in the window guiding her way.

"Anthony?"

She fumbled at the windows, finally got them unbolted. When she flung them open the winds slapped her in the face, bringing her fully awake, fully aware. She was not in the midst of a war waiting for Anthony; she was in the midst of a hurricane awaiting rescue.

The sound that woke her had ceased, and she strained her eyes into the darkness, trying to catch a glimpse of something, anything.

"Annie!" Colt's voice. But where was he? "Over here."

A dark object floated past her window, and beyond she saw the beam of light. A boat, lashed to the magnolia tree, and in it stood Colt Butler.

She gave a whoop of joy. "Thank God, you're here. Can you get the boat any closer?"

"No. Too much risk."

"That's okay." She started over the windowsill.

"Wait! I'll come to you."

"There's no need. I'm a strong swimmer."

"We can't go back in the dark. It's too dangerous. Do you have a flashlight?"

"Yes."

"Get it. Train it over this way. Light me a path, Annie."

He secured the boat, then dived into the dark waters.

A small eternity later he was in the attic. Colt scooped her into his arms and held her close, his heart pounding so hard, the blood roared in his ears.

"I thought you were in New York." He held on to her, unwilling to let go.

"I changed my mind."

"I would have come sooner if I had known."

"You came. That's all that matters."

They swayed together, and never had a woman felt so good to him, so perfect.

"When that helicopter flew in, then left, I thought I was stuck here."

"I said I'd return for you, but of course, you couldn't hear me."

She pulled back to look up at him. "That was you?"

"Yes." She turned pale, and he cupped her face. "Annie . . . what's wrong? Are you all right?"

"It's nothing. I'm fine."

She stepped back from him and wrapped her arms around herself, still pale, suddenly guarded. Colt decided not to pursue the issue. Instead he looked around. In the dim glow of the candle he saw the family portraits lining the far wall. He took in the pallet, the small supply of food and water, the extra batteries she'd brought for the flashlight. He nodded approvingly. Ann Debeau was a smart woman. She hadn't merely retreated; she'd planned ahead.

His eyes fell on the clock, and the roses. Colt was inordinately pleased. He swung his gaze around, looking for the orchids but they were nowhere in sight. That pleased him even more.

He'd caught a glimpse of the card that day in the hallway of Windchime House. To be more precise, he'd sneaked a peak when she wasn't looking. Annie had rescued his roses but had left her fiancé's orchids behind.

"The lights went out before I could get the orchids," she said as if she'd read his mind.

Colt began to whistle. He was with Annie. Nothing could dampen his spirits now.

She moved the roses out of the circle of light. "I don't want you to make anything of it," she said.

"Like what?"

"Never mind. You're dripping wet. We've got to get you out of those clothes."

"I'd like nothing better."

She blushed. "That's not what I meant."

"I like the way your mind works, Miss Annie Debeau."

"Quit calling me that."

"Quit calling you what?"

"Annie."

"It's your name."

"No, it's not. My name is Ann."

"Charlotte Ann Debeau. Annie." Whistling, he made his way to the attic door. Shining the flashlight, he checked the level of water. Ann looked over his shoulder.

"How high was it yesterday?" he asked.

"The third step from the top."

"Good. It's not rising."

"How soon do you think we can leave?"

Only Yesterday

"Not until the storm system has moved on and these floodwaters become less treacherous. It could be a few days." He grinned at her. "Now, what was that you were saying about getting me out of these wet clothes?"

Ann felt selfish to the core. Colt had risked his life to rescue her, and all she could think about was protecting herself. The only excuse she had was temporary insanity.

From the minute he'd stepped into the attic she'd been overcome with an overwhelming sense that she was in some kind of time warp. Every time she looked at him she saw the face in the photograph, Anthony Chance, fighter pilot, artist, her grandmother's lover.

Furthermore, she felt stirrings she'd never felt before, a deep emotional pull that went beyond the physical. Everything about him linked him to the man in the love letters, his looks, his stance, his smile. She'd practically fainted when she found out he was a pilot too.

He was looking at her with that quirky half smile of his, and all she wanted to do was curl against him and be wrapped in his strong arms once more. She'd felt safe there, but more, ever so much more, she'd felt a sense of rightness, of belonging, of fate.

She'd never felt that way in Rob's arms.

The minute that thought entered her mind, she was ashamed of herself. Extraordinary circumstances gave birth to strange emotions, strange behaviors.

Everything would fall into its proper place once she got back to New York.

"I didn't even say thank you for braving those waters to come to me. Please forgive me. I've been incredibly thoughtless."

"There's nothing to forgive. When there's an emergency, I do what I can to help."

His statement was like a dash of cold water. She'd thought his heroics were all for her.

Colt's smile took the sting out of the words. More than that, it made her toes curl and her heart lurch.

It was going to be a long night. Ann turned quickly to the trunk.

"You can't sleep in those wet clothes. There might be something in here that will fit you." She rooted blindly, going more by feel than sight. In the window the candle flickered.

"Here. Let me help you." Colt was beside her, holding a flashlight.

That was the last thing she needed, him kneeling beside her, setting off fireworks underneath her skin. She'd blame her trembling hands on fatigue if she didn't know better.

The beam of the flashlight caught the stack of letters she'd hastily stowed when she went back for the flashlight, and on top, the photograph.

"My God." Colt picked up the picture and held it under the beam of light. "That's unbelievable. Who is this?"

"Anthony Chance."

"Your grandmother's artist."

Only Yesterday

"Her lover."

The words were out before she could stop them. Colt looked as if he'd been shot. He swung the beam of light toward her grandmother's portrait, then back to the photograph.

The silence was electric. So caught up were they in the mystery they'd discovered, they didn't hear the wind pick up speed, didn't hear the distant rumbling of thunder.

Colt cupped her chin and trained the light on her face. "Incredible," he said. "They could be you and me."

"But they aren't," she whispered.

"Do you know that for a fact?" She didn't answer, couldn't answer. "Do you believe in reincarnation, Annie?"

"Don't call me that."

"Why?"

"Because that's what he called her . . . in the letters."

Colt traced her face with the tips of his fingers. "Didn't you feel it, Annie? From the very beginning. There's something special between us."

She shook her head vigorously, trying to deny the truth. But there it was, staring her in the face.

"I won't let it be true."

"You can't stop your feelings any more than you can stop any other powerful force of nature. They're just there, Annie, like the sun rising in the morning or the evening star shining in a darkening sky."

He was still touching her face, and she wanted to

lean into his touch and purr. She wanted to pull him down to the antique quilt and wrap herself around him so close, she couldn't tell where her skin ended and his began. She wanted to make love to him, real love, the kind that built slowly, with hot, lingering kisses and heady explorations.

"What are you thinking?" he said.

She couldn't tell him. She didn't dare.

"I'm thinking that you're going to catch pneumonia and die in those wet clothes." She pulled free and rummaged in the trunk until she came across a pair of pants and a white shirt, vintage, smelling slightly of mothballs.

"These should fit." She thrust them into his hands. "I'll turn my back."

He chuckled as if she'd made a joke. "So, what happened to him? Why didn't they marry?"

"I don't know yet. I've just started reading his letters."

"I'd love to read them . . . if you offered. But of course they're your family history, not mine . . . You can turn around now."

The clothes were a perfect fit. Nervous sweat popped out on her brow.

"From the cut and style I'd guess these were your grandfather's."

"No. He was a very small man. So was my father."

Colt lifted his eyebrow, but she was grateful he didn't speculate. Ann didn't want to think about Anthony Chance anymore. She didn't want to puzzle over the bizarre similarities.

"I'm afraid I can't offer you much in the way of sleeping accommodations. I didn't expect company."

"I'm glad to see you still have your sense of humor."

"Better to laugh than to cry." She handed him the antique quilt.

He took the quilt, and along with it her hand. His eyes never left hers as he planted a kiss in her palm.

"Sweet dreams, Annie."

SEVEN

The night was moonless. Catlike, Colt adjusted to the black void that was the inside of the attic until he could pick out shadows, the old steamer trunk hunkered in the dark like a half-grown sleeping bull, an upright hat-rack where fedoras and top hats and wide-brimmed summer hats sprouted like exotic flowers, the shelf along the west wall where odd-shaped objects crouched like so many cats set to spring, the sleek lines of Annie as she lay sleeping on the pallet within an arm's reach.

He balled his hand into a fist to keep from touching her. His job was to rescue her, not confuse her.

He swung his gaze to the window, heard the steady beat of rain against the panes. With each drop that fell, their chances of leaving the attic tomorrow decreased. The journey to Windchime House had been treacherous. With the floodwaters even more swollen, he wouldn't dare put Annie at risk.

She tossed in her sleep, moaning. Her hand, flung

Only Yesterday

out like a flower, lay in the dark space between their pallets. Colt reached out and with one fingertip traced the pattern of delicate bones across the tops of her fingers, the ridge of her knuckles, downward to the small knob of her wrist. Then turning to his side, he gathered the small hand into his and strained across the darkness to watch her sleep.

A streak of lightning illuminated the attic, bursting silver and gold into the room so that for a moment she flickered into full view, beautiful as a dream, a heartbeat, a memory. Too quickly she lay in darkness once more.

Colt closed his eyes, hoping sleep would claim him, but her cry brought him bolt upright.

"No! The clock, the clock." Still sleeping she thrashed from side to side, fighting the dreams that terrified her.

He rolled over and cradled her close, pressing her head against his chest, holding her arms tightly against his body.

"Shhh. It's okay, Annie. It's only a dream."

She snuggled against him, sighing. Her hand was open against his heart, and he wondered that the pounding didn't awaken her.

He held her that way for a time, listening to the rain and wishing he had a right to be the one she turned to in the night. Strange. He'd never wanted so much from a woman.

Her breath fanned warm against his skin, heating his blood. He pulled his hips back lest the disturbance in his own body convey itself to hers.

Suddenly she was thrashing again, pushing against him.

"No! Anthony . . . Anthony!"

"It's a nightmare, Annie. Nothing more." He tried to soothe her with quiet words, soft caresses, but she jerked upright, eyes wide and staring into the distance as if she were still seeing the images of her dream.

"I can't find him. Anthony!"

He cupped her face, caught the tears that dripped off her chin with the pads of his thumbs. Then he sought to soothe her in the only way he knew how.

"I'm here," he whispered. "I'm right beside you."

She calmed down immediately and leaned against him, breathing in his scent. Feeling like a thief, he slid his hands into her sleek hair, then downward until his thumbs rested in the small, silky indentation at the base of her skull. She lifted her face to his, and he kissed her, softly at first, afraid to shatter the dream. Then as his passion mounted, with growing ardor.

"Annie . . . Annie." He murmured her name, drawing her closer until she was fitted against him as intimately as a lover.

Her mouth flowered open, and he explored the soft inner recesses, the sweet nubby texture of her tongue, the satiny ridges of her inner jaws. Her arms tightened around him, her body tensing like the strings of a piano drawn tight for tuning.

His response was instantaneous. In perfect mimicry of that age-old mating ritual, he thrust his tongue against hers. She arched into him, moaning in pleasure.

Her hands delved under his shirt, splayed against

his back, fingers spread wide, tips pressing into his bare skin. He found the soft mounds of her breasts, circled his thumbs on nipples as erect and tight as rosebuds.

Passion rode him hard. He had to rein it in to keep from lunging into her with the force of a stallion at stud.

Honor held him back. And pride. He didn't want to make love to her as another man. If he loved her—*when* he loved her—it would be as Colt Butler, not as the Anthony Chance of her dreams.

He softened the kiss, then pulled back from her.

"Annie, listen to me." He cupped her face again, feeling the flushed heat of her skin. "You're dreaming."

"If this is a dream, don't wake me, Colt."

Colt? Something like Fourth of July sparklers went off inside his chest.

"When did you realize it was me?"

"From the moment your lips touched mine." She scooted backward onto her pallet and hugged her knees. "I was dreaming, and I felt such a sense of loss." She raked her hands through her dark hair. "Then you were there, and you felt so good, so safe. And when you kissed me, I kissed you back. I'm sorry."

"I'm not."

Breathless, they waited, respecting the small, dark space that separated them.

"I don't mean to mislead you, Colt. I'm committed to Rob."

"And he's in New York and I'm here."

"Please . . . it's not like that. *I'm* not like that."

She flung aside the covers, lit the candle, and set it

on the floor between them. Then she reached for his hand.

"I don't know how to explain this," she said. "I guess I'm doing a very poor job."

"I'm listening."

"I feel connected to you. I don't know why. Maybe it's because you rescued me." She laughed. "Maybe I'm like the captives who fall under the spell of their captors. Or perhaps I owe my life to you because you saved it."

"Maybe the answer is in the letters." He glanced toward the trunk. "When you were dreaming you cried out Anthony Chance's name, but you also kept saying something about a clock."

"A clock? I don't recall reading anything about a clock."

She went to the trunk and took out the stack of letters. Fanned across the floor in the candlelight, they glowed like the faces of ghosts. Sorting through, she found the ones she hadn't read. The brittle paper crackled as she pulled a letter from the envelope.

"My dearest Annie," she read aloud, head bent, shiny hair sliding forward over the left side of her cheek. She glanced up at him to see his reaction.

He felt exalted and humbled at the same time. That she would share private family letters with him demonstrated the deepest sort of trust.

"Thank you," he said.

She merely nodded, then continued reading. "It is morning and all is quiet, but last night the sky was lit up with red tracers and exploding shells. The *Chicago* was hit and so were we, but we got lucky and the torpedo that hit us didn't explode. The *Chicago* sank. Selfish to the core, I was glad it was them and not us. A watery Pacific grave is not in my plans for the future. You are, my darling Annie, and all the babies we will have."

Something lurched inside Colt. "All my love," he whispered.

"That's exactly what it says. How did you know?"

"A lucky guess." She put the letter on the pile, and he picked it up and scanned it. "Nothing about a clock."

She picked up another letter. "My darling," she said, reading aloud. "Death and destruction all around. The only thing that keeps me sane is thinking of you, of the way you look with your hair flowing down your back, of the way you tilt your head back when you laugh, of the way your skin looks like pearls when the sun slants across it. Think of me, Annie. Every time you look at the clock I gave you the day I left . . ."

Annie lifted her face to his. "The clock," she said.

"What else does he say in the letter?"

She continued. ". . . think of the months and weeks and days flying by, think that each minute ticked off draws closer the day when we will be together again."

"That's all?"

"No. There's more." Bright color flagged her cheeks. It was very appealing, that innocent blush.

Colt took the letter and finished reading it, silently, out of respect for her.

"Remember what I told you. 'The clock is to mark time until we meet again.' And when Felix the Cat wags his tail, you ain't seen nothing yet, babe! Just wait till I get home. Your very own ever loving tomcat, Anthony."

Stunned, Colt could do nothing but stare at Ann Debeau, the woman who had inexplicably been his Annie from the moment they met. He recalled the day he'd first seen her, standing on tiptoes to reach the clock. He hadn't known why they were both drawn to the ridiculous cat clock, couldn't have said why he'd bought it for her, why he'd handed it to her in the doorway with the admonition, "To mark time until we meet again."

He laid the letter on the stack between them. "Do you know where the clock is?"

"Maybe it's not the same clock," she said. She went to the trunk and rummaged around, arranging its contents on the floor along with the letters. There was a locket, rose-gold, the engraving worn thin by years of touching.

She snapped it open. Inside were pictures of Charlotte Ann Harris and Anthony Chance.

She brought out a Bible with a tattered cover, a silk shawl with pink roses embroidered on the border, the white dress her grandmother had been painted in.

But no clock.

The candle melted down and flickered. Colt knelt

beside her at the trunk, and their shadows merged on the attic walls.

"We'll look tomorrow when it's light."

Her eyes were bright as she stared at him, then slowly she turned her face to the window.

"It's raining," she said.

"Don't worry. I'll keep you safe."

He held out his hand, and she placed hers softly inside. He led her to the pallet, snuffed out the candle, then lay down beside her, her head cradled on his shoulder.

She drew the antique quilt over them. "Good night, Colt," she said.

" 'Night, dear Annie."

Ann jarred awake at first light. Her face was pressed into the curve of Colt's shoulder, her arm flung across his chest, and her leg pressed tight against his thigh. She felt a twinge of disloyalty to Rob, then quickly shoved it aside.

Comfort. That's all it was. Nothing had happened between her and Colt, nothing at all except that he'd held her close and kept the nightmares at bay.

She untangled herself quietly, softly, then walked barefoot to the window and looked out. A gray sheet of rain obscured everything except the tip of a red fender floating by, and in the distance lightning split the sky.

Ann turned away and freshened up as much as she could. She'd brought toiletries and fresh undergarments, but no clothes. She hadn't expected to be stranded in her attic more than the time it took the hurricane to pass over Fairhope.

Little did she know.

On the pallet, Colt stirred, but his chest rose and fell in the steady rhythm of a deep sleeper.

Ann took her grandmother's white dress out of the trunk, then disappeared behind a folding screen painted with street scenes from Paris.

When she emerged Colt was sitting on the only chair in the attic, a sturdy chaise longue upholstered in red velvet. He whistled, then strode across the floor and took both her hands.

"Wow. Look at you."

The dress was an almost-sheer fabric that felt soft against her skin and floated about her legs when she walked.

"It makes me wish styles hadn't changed so drastically," she said.

"While you were back there doing that magician's act, I poked around some."

With a flourish, he removed a dust cloth from the far end of the shelf. And there it sat, grin intact, pop eyes covered with dust, tail just waiting for the opportunity to wag once more. Felix the Cat.

"Incredible," she whispered. "If it weren't for the dust, I'd think it was the one you gave me."

She stood rooted to the spot, unable to take her eyes off the ancient clock.

"Annie." Colt held out his hand. "Come. Let's see what sort of secrets this old clock can tell us."

As they approached the shelf they saw the gift tag,

still attached, hanging from the cat's tail with a faded yellow ribbon. "To Annie from Anthony, with all my love, forever and always."

"Do you think the clock still works," she whispered, for it seemed almost a sacrilege to speak aloud in the presence of Anthony Chance's gift of love.

"We'll soon know."

Holding tightly to her right hand, Colt lifted the clock off the shelf.

A bolt of lightning struck something outside with a loud crack that shattered the attic window. The room lit up as if it were on fire, and thunder roared louder than a freight train.

She held tightly to Colt's hand, and she could see his mouth working, saying her name, but the sound of it was as faint as if he were calling to her from the other end of a tunnel. Light blinded her, and she thought about closing her eyes, but she didn't want to lose sight of the man who held her hand, the man who had seen her safely through the night and who would surely see her safely through this latest adventure.

She had a floating sensation, as if her body had drifted away and it was taking her mind a while to catch up. The light changed intensity, from a brightness that hurt her eyes to something kinder, softer.

She closed her eyes, just for an instant, and then she felt the sidewalk under her feet and the warmth of the sun on her face.

For a moment she was disoriented. Woolgathering, her mother called it. Daydreaming. She had been guilty of a lot of that lately.

Shaking her head to rid it of the dream-fog, she looked up and there was the sign, New Orleans Public Library.

Smiling, Charlotte Ann Harris opened the door and went inside.

EIGHT

The stacks of books on architecture were on the second floor. Charlotte Ann browsed until she found the one she needed for her project on Victorian houses. She flipped through the pages to make certain, then started back downstairs to check it out when another book caught her attention, this one on the Greek Revival style, volume one of a set of four.

And she wanted to read them all.

Her mother had teased her just last week about her habit of trying to learn everything at once. "You think you can learn everything your freshman year?" she'd said.

Laughing to herself, Charlotte Ann balanced her stack of books and negotiated her way down the aisle. The pile was so tall, she couldn't see over it, so she used the stacks on either side of her as guides.

Suddenly she crashed into a solid object. Books toppled in every direction, and she saw that the solid object was a man. Not just any man but the most gorgeous man she'd ever seen, one so comely that she stood in the library gawking like a teenager.

"I beg your pardon," he said, then knelt at her feet and retrieved the scattered books.

She was too enraptured to move. And besides that, her toes were curling under, a sure sign that fate had more in mind for her than a career as an architect.

Still on his knees, he was in the process of handing her a book when he froze, the picture of a man zapped by Cupid's arrow.

"You are, without a doubt, the most beautiful woman I've ever seen." He pressed the book into her hand, then held on. "I want to kiss you and paint you, in that order."

Like a woman in the middle of her own dream, she knelt on the floor beside him. Hidden from view, he cupped her chin and kissed her full on the lips, softly, tenderly, and she fell totally, irrevocably in love.

The kiss lasted no more than a few seconds, but it was enough. From the moment he touched her, she knew he was the love of her life, that whatever else happened, she would always love this man.

"What is your name?" he asked.

"Charlotte Ann Harris."

He turned her face from side to side, studying it from all angles.

"I'll call you Annie," he said.

"And what will I call you?"

"I've been told that men who fall in love become

besotted to the point that they forget everything they ever knew, including manners. Forgive me."

He planted a soft kiss in her palm, and she felt the fever of his lips spread through her entire body. Charlotte Ann was amazed, but not afraid. She didn't know much about love and romance. Her father had died when she was eight, and her mother somehow never got around to explaining the ways of the birds and the bees.

"My name is Anthony Chance." More than six feet tall, he towered over Charlotte Ann. And when he smiled down at her, she felt as if a god on Mount Olympus were granting her favor.

He carried her books with one hand and kept the other on the small of her back, gently guiding her. And Charlotte Ann Harris, who had never let anybody tell her what to do, not even her mother, allowed herself to be propelled through the stacks by this handsome stranger.

"Where do you live?" he asked when they were on the sidewalk.

Independent from the top of her head to the tip of her toes, she always maintained her distance from the boys who tried to court her until she decided how much of her private life she wanted to reveal to them. Which was usually little if any.

But this Anthony Chance was no boy. And he certainly wasn't the kind of man who would wait politely for her to make up her mind just how the courtship would go.

Charlotte Ann was secretly pleased. Until she had

met him she was beginning to think all men were so much putty, she could mold any way she wanted. And of course, Laura Ellen was no help at all in the matter.

"Boys will be boys," was her mother's sole comment on the opposite sex.

"St. Charles. Garden District," she told Anthony. "Why?"

"Because I'm going home to meet your parents."

"Parent. It's just my mother and me. Two against the world is the way she puts it."

"And how would you put it?"

"One swept along by events, the other standing with heels dug in defying the world at every turn."

He laughed. "The latter would be you."

"How do you know?"

He set her books down, then caught her around the waist and swung her aboard the streetcar.

"The way you hold your chin, square and upright, determined." He sat beside her, close enough so that their thighs were touching. "What I don't already know about you, Annie Harris, I intend to find out."

The bell clanged, the car rattled, and they were off. Anthony lifted her hand and boldly branded her palm with another kiss, in broad daylight with six people in the back of the car looking on.

Charlotte Ann thought it was altogether appropriate that they were riding on a streetcar named Desire.

Her mother was everything Anthony had imagined, beautiful, charming, and totally dependent on her strong-willed daughter to give her life meaning and direction.

They sat in the parlor on three velvet-covered Victorian chairs so small that Anthony's knees were practically touching his chest. The parlor was an ultrafeminine woman's room full of bric-a-brac and lace doilies and heavy velvet draperies that shut out the sun.

The first thing Annie did when they arrived was fling open the curtains so the sun streamed inside and they had a view of the courtyard beyond the French doors.

Anthony fell in love with her all over again. Though he should have been uncomfortable with his knees stuck practically under his chest, he was supremely at ease, a man who had finally found what he'd been searching for all his life.

The funny thing was, until he saw Annie he hadn't even known he was searching. All he'd known was a restlessness that took him from city to city, filling canvases like mad, painting from five in the morning till midnight sometimes, like someone possessed. And in between painting sprees he was on the water racing his sailboat or up in the air pushing his little plane to the limits, testing himself to see just how far he could go.

"Mr. Chance, I can't tell you how honored I am to have you in our home." Laura Ellen Harris sat with her legs primly crossed at the ankles and her hands folded in her lap, the picture of decorum. "I've seen your work, and I think it's marvelous."

"Thank you, Mrs. Harris. And call me Anthony, please."

"Oh, I couldn't possibly. That's far too informal for a man of your stature."

"What about for a son-in-law?"

Laura Ellen nearly dropped her teacup, but Annie merely smiled. She'd known from the moment they met, just as he had. It pleased Anthony that she wasn't going to play silly, time-consuming games with him.

"I intend to be your son-in-law, Mrs. Harris. I've come today to ask for your daughter's hand in marriage."

Laura Ellen turned to her daughter. "Charlotte Ann, you haven't told me a thing about this. Why, you've never even mentioned his name."

"That's because we just met, Mother."

Laura Ellen patted her face with a lace handkerchief. "It's just like you to keep things a secret. You met last month at that cotillion, I suppose."

"No. Today. In the library."

"I just don't know what to say. If I were the swooning kind, I'd swoon."

Annie laughed heartily, then left her chair, planted a kiss on her mother's cheek, and fondly ruffled her hair.

"You are the swooning kind, Mother. Only you're too curious right now to swoon."

"I am curious."

"I hope I haven't caused you undue stress, Mrs. Harris. When I want something I don't beat around the bush, I go after it."

Annie patted her mother's hand. "Don't worry, Mother. I plan to lead him a merry chase before I let him catch me."

"Charlotte Ann! Where's your gentility?"

Anthony laughed. "I fully intend to marry your daughter, Mrs. Harris, but not without a courtship. I want to give you plenty of time to get to know me."

"What about me? Don't you plan to give me time to get to know you?" Annie said, grinning.

"We knew each other the moment we met, Annie."

True to his word, Anthony began a courtship of Annie the next day.

When she left her classes, he was parked on campus outside the architecture building.

"Fancy seeing you here," she said, leaning against his car.

He opened the door for her, and without even asking where they were going, she stepped inside. He drove effortlessly, as he seemed to do everything.

"I'm going to paint you today."

"That wouldn't be a ploy to get me to pose nude, would it?" Her smile told him she was teasing.

The sidelong glance he gave her made her sizzle, and she wondered what demons had made her bring up a subject that was sure to lead down a dangerous pathway. But then, she'd never been one to run from danger.

"When you're nude, Annie, you won't be posing."

"*When?*"

"That's right. *When.*"

"You're awfully sure of yourself, Anthony Chance."

"I'm awfully sure of you, Annie."

"That has to be boring. I thought men loved the chase."

"Games are for fools. I love substance, not silly pretense."

They drove to the river, and there he set up his easel and painted Annie, sitting on a patchwork quilt beside the water, head bent over her books, long hair sliding across one rosy, sunlit cheek.

It was like that for a week. Every day when she got out of class, he was waiting for her. Sometimes they strolled around campus, hand in hand. Other times they drove along River Road with the top down through avenues of live oak trees dripping with Spanish moss.

Charlotte Ann lay awake in her bed at night, eyes wide open, heart pounding double time, heat spreading through her body, dreaming of him. Though she was a virgin, she wasn't naive. She understood her symptoms. She wanted Anthony Chance. It was that simple.

What wasn't simple was making a decision to do something about it. The mores of her time dictated that young women of virtue remain virgins till they were married. Women who did not earned names and reputations that embarrassed their families.

Charlotte Ann had never been bound by convention, but she'd never flouted convention in any way that would be considered immoral.

She kicked aside her sheets and flung open her window to let the night breezes cool her off. Her relief was only temporary. The minute she was back in bed she was thinking of Anthony, wanting him, needing him.

Why was it that men could do just about anything they wanted and society wouldn't raise an eyebrow, but women were branded immoral for the same acts? Feeling defiant and frustrated and more than a little angry, Charlotte Ann slid deeper under the covers.

Laura Ellen was waiting for her at the breakfast table in the sunroom the next morning.

"Have you thought about a date for the wedding?" she said.

"I'd marry him tomorrow if he asked me to."

"Charlotte Ann! What would people say. Everybody in polite society would call it a shotgun wedding."

"I don't give a fig for polite society."

"I know you don't, but I do." Laura Ellen spread an assortment of magazines on the table. "What I was getting at earlier, is that we're going to need at least a year to plan this wedding." She flipped rapidly through the pages. "Now here's the latest fashion in wedding gowns."

The doorbell rang, and joy flooded Charlotte Ann. "Whatever you want, Mother. You plan it."

She kissed her mother's cheek, raced toward the

door, then raced back and grabbed three pieces of buttered toast with orange marmalade.

"Might need something for energy," she said.

Anthony's upstairs apartment in the French Quarter overlooked the St. Louis Cathedral. The minute they arrived Annie threw open all the doors and windows then stood on the balcony with her face tipped up to the sun and her arms spread wide.

"Glorious," she said, smiling at him over her shoulder.

"It certainly is," he agreed, but he wasn't talking about the view from the balcony. Annie was the most appealing woman he'd ever met, a rare combination of wholesome innocence and heady sex appeal. Stopping at a kiss was increasingly difficult for him. And in the privacy of his apartment, he dared not risk even a simple kiss.

"Listen," she said. "Hear that. The birds are singing as they fly around the bell tower." She laughed. "If I could sing I'd join them."

He slid his arms around her waist, and she leaned against his shoulder.

"What would you sing, Annie?"

"A happy song. You make me very happy, Anthony."

"It works both ways."

She swayed, keeping time with the song of the birds and the song in her mind, and that small movement caused his libido to riot.

"We should start packing that picnic lunch if we want to go sailing." He started pulling back, and she turned to face him.

"What do you want, Anthony, right this very minute?"

"You."

She held him spellbound with a long, deep look, then she turned her face upward, toward the crystal bowl of a sky, as if she could find the answer she searched for there. When she turned back to him, he could see resolve in her eyes, in the set of her jaw, in every line of her body.

"Make love to me, Anthony."

He'd heard that the wonder of love can sometimes make a man's heart stand still, but until that moment he hadn't known it was true.

"You don't know what you ask, Annie."

"I may be naive and totally innocent, but I know exactly what I want and what I'm asking."

She took both his hands and lifted them to her breasts. Her blouse and the camisole underneath were the softest batiste, and he could feel the tight budding of her nipples underneath. He closed his eyes, stealing the moment, reveling in this forbidden touch.

Abruptly he broke contact. "I won't sully your reputation."

"You want to take a virgin to your wedding bed. Is that it?"

God, how she could challenge a man.

"I want to take you to my wedding bed, Annie. The rest is irrelevant to me."

"To me, as well."

She swept past him through the French doors, then stood in a bright patch of sunlight and unbuttoned her blouse. He watched from the safe distance of the balcony, mesmerized.

Not that the nude female body was new to him. He'd used it as a subject for his passion as well as his art. But he'd never been in love. And love made the difference.

Annie stripped the camisole off, then stood before him, creamy breasts tipped as pink as camellia blossoms.

"You tempt me so, Annie."

Her eyes riveted on his, she unfastened her skirt and it slithered to the floor. Then hooking her thumbs into the elastic waistband, she peeled off her half-slip and her panties.

"My God. You are the most beautiful woman I've ever seen."

"I'm yours. Come and claim me."

"Don't think I don't want to."

"The thing you should know about me, Anthony, is that I'm not bound by convention. I don't care a fig what people say about me as long as I can look at myself in the mirror and be proud of what I've done." With slow, languorous movements she lifted her hair off her neck, arched her back, then released the silken mass to let it cascade over her shoulders.

It was the sexiest gesture Anthony had ever witnessed, on-screen or off.

"Annie, if you don't put your clothes back on, I won't be responsible for what I might do."

"And what would that be?" She ran her tongue slowly around her lush lips.

"Minx. Keep that up and you'll find out."

"Promises, promises."

He anchored himself to the balcony by catching hold of the wrought-iron railing. She laughed, then blew him a pouty kiss. He sought to lighten the mood with humor.

"Do you have a secret life down on Bourbon Street as the Queen of Erotica?"

"No. I have a secret life as a woman in love who has to give herself relief in the darkness under the covers, clamping her teeth onto her bottom lip so her mother sleeping in the next room won't hear."

Her total honesty disarmed him. Her courage enchanted him. She wasn't merely defying society and disdaining their rules: She was giving herself completely to him in an act of love and trust that both stunned and humbled him.

He strode through the French doors, wrapped his arms around her, and buried his face in her hair.

"Annie, my darling, my love."

"What took you so long?" she whispered.

"I was adjusting to the reality that I've fallen in love with a woman who is both braver and smarter than I am."

"Flattery will get you everywhere."

"I don't speak pretty lies, I speak the truth."

She stood on tiptoe and pressed her mouth to his,

and he was lost. She was silk and heat and sweet surrender, and he savored her the way he would a vintage wine that had been kept in storage until it reached the point of perfection.

Fully aroused, his body cried for release, but he had to be absolutely certain that Annie knew what she asked of him.

Lifting his head, he studied her face. "Unless you tell me no, I'm going to take you to my bed and claim every delicious inch of you, not merely your body, but your heart and soul."

"You've already claimed two out of three." Her laugh was a little shaky, but determination was written in every line of her body, from the upward-tilting chin to the pert thrust of her breasts. "The first moment I saw you, I knew you were my soul mate. The ceremony will come in time, but in the stacks at the library we were joined as surely as if a priest had said the vows."

She kissed the side of his jaw, then his mouth. "Love me, Anthony."

Anthony carried her across the threshold of his bedroom, an act fraught with symbolism, for today in his sunlit apartment she was leaving behind the innocence of her youth and entering a realm of joy given only to those who truly love.

Her eyes widened when he laid her on the bed and stripped off his clothes.

"Don't be afraid, Annie."

"I'm not afraid."

"You can still change your mind."

"I won't."

Smiling, she lifted her arms to him, and he fell into heaven.

Annie had dreamt of this moment ever since she'd met Anthony Chance, but her dreams paled beside the reality. He was smoke and fire, stroking her skin until she smoldered. He was music and poetry, singing through her veins with the melodies of an exultation of larks. He was thunder and wind, sweeping her into a storm of passion that took her breath away.

He trailed his fingers lightly across her throat, pausing where her pulse fluttered like the wings of a butterfly, then downward where he massaged her nipples until she was in a frenzy of wanting.

"Anthony, please," she cried out, wanting more and yet hardly knowing what it was she longed for.

"Patience, my sweet Annie. Love is best when savored."

With fingertips and tongue he sensitized the skin of her belly, her inner thighs, behind her knees, in the blue-veined arch of her foot. She felt as if the strings of a thousand violins were vibrating just under her skin.

He slid his fingers into her soft, wet folds, and she arched as waves of pleasure spiraled upward. Then he pressed his mouth over her, kissing her deeply, moving his tongue so that she grew wild with wanting.

Instinctively she began to move, undulating her hips in perfect rhythm with his tongue. Heat built to the point of explosion, and she clenched around him, trying to get control of the pleasure that threatened to rip her apart.

"Go with it, Annie," he whispered, his voice hoarse with desire. "Go with the flow."

"I think I'm going to die of this joy."

She gave in to the sensations, let them rocket her to the stars and back. Bent over her, Anthony smiled, and she reached for him, needing to anchor herself lest she fly off and never come back.

"I never dreamed it would be so wonderful," she whispered.

"The best is yet to come." He smoothed her damp hair back from her face. "I'll be as gentle with you as I can, but this may hurt a little."

"As long as I have you, nothing can hurt me, Anthony."

Lionlike, he poised above her, the tip of his shaft resting lightly in her soft, moist folds. Need clawed at her, and she lunged upward, wanting to discover all the mysteries at once.

He pulled his hips back. "Patience, my love, patience."

Slowly he slid his shaft into her, and flowerlike, she received him, sweet, hot petals unfurling by degrees. She held her breath, suspended by the beauty and the awe of this sacred act.

He thrust slowly, shallowly, meeting her resistance, then pulling back. Sensations spiraled through her, and Annie felt as if she'd sprouted wings.

"Relax, darling . . . That's it."

Only Yesterday

He thrust deeply, and she felt a quick stab of pain . . . then heaven.

"Are you all right?" he said.

She smiled at him, as satisfied as a cat who has been let loose in the creamery. "If I were any better, I'd fly," she said.

"I can't have you doing that. I have plans for you."

"What are they?"

"Do you really want me to tell you?"

"Why don't you show me?"

And he did. The sun made changing patterns on the sheets, and the birds serenaded from their perch on the balcony. But Anthony and Annie were oblivious to everything except each other. He took her to the edge and back repeatedly while the sky changed from the blue of a robin's egg to the paint-box colors of a Mardi Gras parade.

She felt damp and lush and sated, and still Anthony loved. Just when she thought she had no more to give, a hurricane built inside her, and she was ripped out of her languorous state into a cataclysmic sensation that left her mindless.

Sweat rolled down Anthony's face, and his eyes darkened as if all light had been extinguished from within.

"Now," he cried out, and a volcanic stream shot through her as she spasmed.

He held her close, rolling to his side so his weight wouldn't crush her, silently stroking her hair. Annie lay in his arms, boneless and speechless while soft music from the radio on the bedside table wafted over her.

She would never forget the song as long as she lived—"It Had To Be You."

"They're playing our song," Anthony whispered. "I love you, Annie. Forever and always."

She joined their palms and laced her fingers through his. "Till death do us part, Anthony Chance."

They had supper at a small café two blocks from his apartment, huge buns dripping with olive oil and stuffed with three kinds of meat and two kinds of cheese. They'd missed lunch, and they were ravenous.

Afterward they joined hands and strolled through the French Quarter, looking in shop windows.

Annie saw it first, the little black clock, cat-shaped, complete with rolling eyes and wagging tail.

"He's adorable." She tugged Anthony's hand. "Let's go inside and see."

The shop bell tinkled when they entered.

"May I help you?" The owner was a graying matron with a wide smile that showed two gold teeth. She introduced herself as Marvelene.

"We'd like to see the clock, please," Anthony said.

Marvelene pulled the clock off the shelf and held it toward them. Annie touched the smooth black surface, and energy pulsed through her. Squeezing Anthony's hand, she traced the sassy smile on the cat's face.

The room whirled, and she closed her eyes against the dizziness. Too much excitement, she decided. After all, it wasn't every day a girl became a woman.

She turned to ask Anthony to take her back to the

apartment, when the sky lit up. Thunder rumbled, and that was the only warning they had of the storm that lashed the city. A blanket of gray rain obscured the shop door, the sidewalks, the buildings beyond.

A brilliance flashed across the sky once more, and Annie gathered electrical force from the air that swirled around her like fog. She closed her eyes, floating.

"Anthony . . ." She knew she'd called out to him, but the sound of her own voice was but a distant echo. Tightly she clung to his hand. As long as he was by her side, everything would be all right.

"Take me back," she whispered, and then she felt herself falling, and strong arms reaching out to catch her.

NINE

"I've been waiting for you to come around," he said.

Her mind a jumble, Ann kept her eyes tightly closed, her hand clutching the clock. There had been a wonderful afternoon in Anthony's apartment, and then the stroll along Royal Street, and the quaint little shop with the clock, then the terrible lightning storm.

"Annie." She felt his hand caress her cheek.

There was no mistaking his voice.

"Anthony?"

Slowly she opened her eyes. Images came to her in jagged flashes—Anthony smiling at her, brilliant light, a roaring sound, ticking of a clock, the portrait Anthony painted, an old trunk, yellowing letters, a tender touch, his lips on hers.

For a moment she let herself savor the kiss, then she pulled away.

"Colt?"

"It's me, Annie."

Only Yesterday

"What happened?"

"Don't you know?" he said.

"No." She brushed her hair back from her flushed cheeks. She remembered putting on the dress from the trunk, remembered Colt pointing out the clock, remembered the bright flashes of lightning that filled the room, shattered the attic window. And then . . .

"I'm so tired," she said. "Did I faint?"

"No, you didn't faint." Colt chuckled. "You're not the fainting kind."

"There's always a first time, you know."

Why was he so chipper? And why did her heart lurch and her skin flush every time she looked at him, as if they'd spent the night together in the throes of deep passion instead of stranded in the attic, sleeping sedately side by side, keeping each other company in the storm?

"What you are, Annie, is a woman of great courage, a woman who is not afraid to defy convention."

Colt made it sound like a compliment. She wished Rob felt that way.

"I am unconventional," she admitted. "Even for New York."

He threw back his head when he laughed, and there was something so familiar about the gesture and the full-bodied sound of mirth that Ann shivered.

"I'm not talking about New York." He began to hum, then sing, "It Had To Be You."

Ann felt elated and scared all at the same time, and though it was stuffy in the attic, she wrapped her arms around herself to stop shivering.

"Nice song," she said.

"Our song," he said.

Ann stood up so fast, she dropped the clock. Colt caught it in midair, then set it back on the dusty attic shelf. She walked to the window for a breath of fresh air, expecting to see broken glass scattered across the floor. Instead, the window was intact.

Before her strange blackout she'd distinctly heard the sound of shattering glass. She pushed open the window, then leaned out for deep gulps of fresh air.

The rain had stopped, and a watery-looking sun was trying to break through the gray clouds. Could it be her imagination, or had the water receded some?

"Annie." She jumped when Colt put his hand on her shoulder. "Are you all right?"

His kindness was her undoing. She whirled on him, fury written in every line of her body.

"Am I all right! How can you ask such a thing? I'm stranded in the attic, half of Fairhope is floating past my window, I'm hungry and tired and scared, and I keep calling you the name of my grandmother's lover."

Tears streamed down her cheeks, though she was not the weeping kind. He reached to touch her cheek, and she swatted his hand away.

"Don't touch me. Don't you dare touch me."

"All right. I won't touch you." He went to their food supply and opened a box of toaster pastries. "Not yet, Annie."

"And stop calling me Annie." Her hands shook as she tucked a strand of hair behind her ear. "My name is Ann Debeau and I live in New York and make my liv-

Only Yesterday

ing as a potter and I'm going to marry a perfectly wonderful man."

He offered her a pastry. "Breakfast?"

"How can you say that?"

"Because I'm starving. Aren't you?"

"What do you think?" She jerked a pastry out of his hand and bit off a chunk that would choke a horse. That's how mad she was. Every ounce of good breeding she'd had vanished, and she was acting like the sort of selfish, testy woman she despised.

"How can you stand there grinning like a possum?" she said.

"New York hasn't taken all the South out of you yet."

"Give it time. Rob says it will."

"He wants you to change?"

"Only for the better."

"He must be a fool."

"He's a decent, hardworking man with a very successful law practice."

"Do you love him?"

She held up her ring finger. "I'm going to marry him."

"You didn't answer my question. Do you love him?"

Ann bought time by munching on her pastry. Did she love Rob? She'd thought so before she came to Fairhope. But lately, she'd wondered the same thing herself.

Face it, she thought. What kind of woman describes the man she loves as merely *decent, hardworking, successful*? Where were all the adjectives her grandmother had used for Anthony Chance in her letters? Magnificent. Wonderful. Magical. Glorious.

The truth hit her with the force of a hammer blow to the midriff: She didn't really love Rob, not in the way of a woman who pledges "to love, honor, and cherish till death us do part."

And yet she'd been brought up to honor commitments. Torn by loyalty and the unmistakable desire that welled up inside her every time she looked at Colt, Ann walked to the window and stood looking out at the aftermath of the storm.

For now her survival depended not only on Colt Butler, but on her own inner strength and courage. She couldn't afford to get sidetracked by volatile emotional issues.

Turning back to him, she said quietly, "You have no right to ask that question."

"I have every right, Annie." He closed the space between them and captured both her hands. "I am Anthony Chance."

TEN

"Impossible," she said.

Colt's statement was almost as shocking to him as it was to Ann. He could no more explain what had happened to them than she could. But he had a bone-deep conviction that whatever they had experienced was life-changing, and more than a hunch that the dreamlike trance he'd found himself in when Annie had collapsed in his arms had something to do with time travel.

His memories were too vivid to be mere dreams—meeting Annie for the first time in the library, riding the streetcar, painting her as she sat on the banks of the river, making love to her on the sun-dappled bed.

But more than the memories was the strength of his feelings for her. Colt loved Ann Debeau, had loved her from the moment they met.

He had known her in another lifetime. It was that simple. And that scary.

He reached for her hand, but she snatched it away.

"I'm sorry to upset you, Annie. I shouldn't have blurted it out like that."

"No, you shouldn't have. Your claim is outrageous."

"I thought all artists believed in magic, Annie."

"The magic of the muse, yes. But you're not talking about inspiration that comes from a mystical source, you're talking about something far more complex."

"Is it?" Colt crossed to the window and studied the havoc nature had wrought. "Look at this, Annie."

She joined him at the window, careful to stand so that no part of her body was touching his. Water raged past just below the windowsill, gray and angry, full of the trash that civilized society generates.

"If you had stood at this window a few days ago, what would you have seen?" he said.

"You know as well as I do—trees, grass, flower beds, the street, streetlights, a sidewalk, a sloping hill down to the bay."

"Is what I propose any more mysterious or magical than this?" Colt's sweeping gesture encompassed the flood-swollen bay that covered the city of Fairhope.

"A hurricane is one of nature's phenomenons."

"How do you know time travel is not another of nature's phenomenons?"

Impatiently she left the window and wandered back to the trunk.

"Because I'm an artist, you think I should embrace this theory without question?"

"No. Not without question. I question it myself.

But everything that has happened to us supports my theory that somehow you and I traveled through time."

She held up her hand as if she could ward off the truth. If he persisted in this line of thought, he risked losing her. But if he didn't convince her that there was a compelling reason for her to reconsider her relationship with Rob, he would lose her anyway.

"Most of us are bound by a conception of time as linear," he said.

"I've done some reading in that field, Colt. It's not that I don't believe what you say is possible. It's simply that I can't accept it as a possibility for you and me."

He didn't ask why: He thought he knew the answer.

"Rome wasn't built in a day," he said.

That brought a smile from her. "Smart man."

He put the box of toaster pastries back on the shelf with their supplies.

"The sun's moving on, Annie, if we could see it. What do you want to do with this day?"

"How about a rousing game of chess? I think I saw a set up here somewhere."

"You've just named my game. Prepare to surrender, Miss Ann Debeau."

She found not only a chess set, but a checkerboard as well. Ann was grateful for the diversion. Anything to keep her mind off the things he had said.

In her art she relied heavily on her instincts. She accepted magic without question. She reveled in the mysterious, the fanciful, the whimsical.

But in her personal life, unconventional though she was, she still tried to keep everything balanced and in some semblance of order. A sense of normality was her anchor. Otherwise she sometimes felt as if she might break into a million pieces and fly off into space.

"Checkmate," Colt said. "That makes four games I've won."

"Don't get cocky. I'm having an off day. That's all." She grinned impishly at him. "Besides, I haven't been cheating."

"You cheat?"

"Not exactly. But sometimes I make up my own rules."

"I've always admired a woman who wasn't afraid to live by her own rules."

"Don't do that."

"What?"

"Keep heaping outrageous compliments on me."

"Why?"

"You know why," she said quietly as she began to gather the games.

The candles they'd lit cast shadows on the walls, and outside the water rushed by in the darkness as if it were on some errand that required haste.

He reached across the chessboard and covered her hand.

"Annie . . . Look at me."

He had the kind of eyes a woman could drown in if she weren't careful. And Ann was feeling more than a little reckless.

"Don't you want to know what happened? Aren't you curious?"

"Yes, I'm curious."

More than curious. She was fascinated, but it was the same kind of fascination that drew a moth to his death in a flame.

"Remember the H. G. Wells stories," he said. "Time travelers always climbed inside a machine."

Ann knew where the conversation was leading. She knew she should pull back, both physically and mentally, but there was comfort in his touch, and magic, a magic she couldn't ignore.

"I think the clock was the key," he added.

"You're saying that when we touched the clock, we went back in time?"

"Maybe. But I think there was more." He turned her hands over and traced the pattern of lines, then lifted them and planted an openmouthed kiss in each of her palms.

There are some things in life that you learn, and some that you simply know. Ann knew the kiss was right. Reason might try to deny it, but her heart knew the truth.

"Are you saying what I think you're saying?"

"What do you think I'm saying, Annie?"

"That we wanted to go back."

"Yes."

Mesmerized, they studied each other. The candlelight cast them in gold, and dust collected over the years rose like mist from the attic floor. Softly, Colt kissed her hand once more, then released her and strode to the darkened shelves, plucked off the old clock, and set it on the floor between them. In the candlelight the cat looked alive. Its tail wagged steadily, and one eye winked at them.

"We both wanted to know the truth, Annie. But I think there's more we need to learn."

She couldn't move, could barely breathe.

"This is all speculation," she whispered. "Sheer madness."

"I agree. Wonderful, remarkable madness."

He put one hand on the black plastic head and held the other toward her, palm up. Slowly, Ann stretched out her hand.

She felt the energy even before her fingertips touched his, and then she was swirling through mists, hurtling through time and space.

From a distance she heard him calling her name, "Annie . . ." He was saying something else, something she could barely hear.

"I'm here, Annie, and I won't ever let you go."

ELEVEN

In her dreams Charlotte Ann was tumbling through space, free-falling, without a safety net to catch her. She cried out, then sat straight up, eyes wide, heart pounding.

Strong arms circled her waist.

"I'm here, Annie, and I won't ever let you go."

She looked up into the dear smiling face of Anthony Chance, and suddenly her world righted.

"I shouldn't have eaten all that apple pie. Too much sugar made me sleepy." She raked her long hair behind one ear. "Why didn't you wake me up? I hate to sleep and miss everything."

"I love to watch you sleeping, and you haven't missed a thing." Anthony took her hands and pulled her up. "This is where we'll build our house, Annie."

They had come to Fairhope for the weekend. Leaving behind the crowded streets of New Orleans, they'd driven as far as Mobile Bay, then boarded his boat and sailed across the waters to the most perfect spot in all of south Alabama.

Shading her eyes with her hands, she studied the land they'd chosen—the green hill that sloped down to the sea where boats with sails unfurled glided by as effortlessly as angels flying; the copse of hardwood trees with branches fanned out, canopylike, over the Johnny-jump-ups and the wild roses; the endless blue sky dotted with puffy white clouds.

"Yes," she said. "It's perfect."

"So are you." Anthony bent over her hand and kissed it.

"You've just made my toes curl under."

"Thank God."

He threw his head back when he laughed, and backlit by the sun he looked like someone she'd imagined, a dream man who had come to her in the dusty stacks of the public library in New Orleans.

"What would you have done if your toes hadn't curled under that day we met?" He had a knack for reading her thoughts.

"What would I have done?" She kicked off her shoes and walked away from him, swinging her skirts and smiling at him over her shoulder, teasing him. "I would have walked away, just like this."

Then she began to run. Her hair blew behind her, and the wind caught her skirts so that they billowed around her like an umbrella.

She heard footsteps pounding behind her, and the sound of his laughter, then she felt his strong arms around her waist. He pulled her down onto the grass, and she tumbled into his arms, her nose buried in his neck as she inhaled the fresh, masculine scent of him. She breathed deeply, as if she could absorb him by smell.

"You smell like spring," she said.

He tangled his hands in her hair and rubbed his nose over her skin, starting with her temples and ending with the indentation at the base of her neck.

"You smell like rose petals." Propping himself on his elbows he gazed down at her. "Did you know that rose petals are edible?"

She loved it when his eyes darkened like that. Her own passion stirred in response, and she held up her arms to him.

"Taste me," she said.

And he did, starting with the tender skin at her throat and working his way slowly downward. On that sunswept hill in the middle of summer with nothing but birds as their witness, they pledged their love for each other in a dozen ways, all of them exquisite, exciting, and erotic.

So eager was she for his touch that Annie helped him with the tiny buttons on her bodice, though he needed no help at all. He had the sensitive, skilled fingers of an artist.

He traced the soft contours of her breasts, his fingers as familiar with her silky skin as her own. She arched her back, and, cupping her breasts, offered them to him, nipples peaked as hard as diamonds. He laved her with his tongue, then closed his mouth over her and suckled.

Moaning deep in her throat, she circled her arms around him and pulled him close.

"I don't ever want this to stop," she whispered. "I don't ever want to let you go."

Lifting onto his elbow, he gazed down at her, the tumbled hair, the flushed cheeks, the bright eyes.

"I want to paint you this way."

She felt like a piano wire strung too tightly. In the stillness of the summer she could almost hear her body humming, crying out for release.

"First, love me."

"I do love you, Annie. Forever and always." He captured her lips, spent a small eternity tasting their sweetness, then moved his attention back to her breasts.

She murmured his name over and over, "Anthony, my love."

"I want you, Annie. Now."

She lifted her skirts, and they flared around her like the petals of some exotic flower. And there on the windswept hill where they would build their house, Charlotte Ann Harris and Anthony Chance merged bodies, minds, and hearts.

When the sun began its descent, flinging banners of rose and gold and purple across the sky, Anthony set up his easel and took out his paints.

"Where shall I sit?" she said.

"I want you standing. You're too strong a woman to paint sitting down."

"Let me rephrase that question. Where shall I stand?"

Only Yesterday

"There." He pointed to the highest peak of the hill, presided over by a solitary magnolia with a trunk wider than the girth of three fat men and with huge white blossoms perfuming the air. "Stand there facing the sea."

The wind caught her hair and her skirt as she turned her face to the sea.

"Perfect." He made the first brush stroke on canvas. "You're standing exactly where we'll build our house."

"How long will this take?"

"Forever."

"I'm serious. How long?"

"I plan to paint you in all your moods, in all the stages of your life, of our life together." His paintbrush moved swiftly on the canvas. "Forever," he said with great conviction.

Overlooking the bay, watching people from Mobile and New Orleans sail toward the summer cottages that dotted the shoreline, Annie imagined what her life would be like, married to Anthony and living in Fairhope, Alabama.

They'd discussed children one sultry night in the French Quarter not long after they met.

"I'm going to sing at our wedding," he'd said.

"Is this a formal proposal?"

"Not yet. When I propose I'm going to do it in grand style, with moonlight and music, riding in a carriage with the fringe on top."

"Suppose I say no?" She loved to tease him. Saying

no to this man was as far from her mind as traveling to the moon.

"You won't."

"You're right. I won't." She sipped her mint julep. "Do you want children?"

"I want you. Everything else is icing on the cake."

The band struck up "It Had To Be You," and reaching across the table, Anthony took her hand and sang the song in a baritone well enough so that he could have a career in music.

She told him so.

"You're prejudiced."

"Guilty," she'd said, laughing, and now standing on the knoll where someday their house would be built, she felt her heart swell with such love, she feared it might burst.

"I never tire of painting your face. You never hide your feelings, Annie. What were you thinking?"

"That you'd made me a fallen woman."

"Liar," he said, teasing her. "You were thinking about the night I proposed."

"How did you know?"

"Magic."

"You're magic, all right." She stalked him.

"Annie. Wait. What are you doing? I'm not finished with you."

She wrapped her arms around him, then her right leg, decadent, shameless, and so very much in love.

"I'm not finished with you, either, Anthony Chance."

His protests turned to kisses, then passion that they

Only Yesterday

played out underneath the canopy of the giant magnolia tree. By the time they were sated, the sun had dropped into the bay, leaving behind a purple dusk that softened the land and turned the trees to ghostly sentinels.

"We'll build our bedroom there," Anthony said, pointing just beyond the magnolia, "with our bed facing this tree so that every time we look out our window, we'll remember this moment."

"Yes," she said. "But I don't need a tree as a reminder, my love. I'll remember this moment and all our moments together, always."

Annie was so young, and still had her architectural schooling in front of her. If it hadn't been for the events unfolding in Europe, Anthony would have waited until she was almost out of college before he started the house. He would have waited until she was only months away from her degree, instead of years, to lay the foundation of their future home.

But in a world threatened with madness, he wanted stability. He wanted a place to come home to, a place where he could picture Annie waiting for him at the window.

There were naysayers who predicted that the United States would never be involved in the war, that Roosevelt would never agree to committing America to the struggle. Isolationist Colonel Charles Lindbergh took to the airwaves in praise of Nazi Germany's "sense of decency," calling Hitler "undoubtedly a great man."

But Anthony sensed something different, an insidious evil that would spread like cancer, encompassing them all. Like all great artists, Anthony followed his heart, listened to his inner voice, and all his intuitions were telling him that his time with Annie would be brief.

Using his summer cottage in Fairhope as a base, he built her house that summer, a house she designed, a house they would fill with love.

And she was by his side, wearing a hard hat and a pair of her daddy's old combat boots, white dress swirling about her legs, long hair blowing in the breezes off the bay, looking as feminine as if she were decked out in dancing shoes for a ball.

As the carpenter nailed the last rafter into place Annie squeezed Anthony's hand.

"Can you believe it?" she said. "It seems like only yesterday the house was a dream, and now look at this." Lifting her skirts, she raced around the skeleton of the house, spinning and twirling in each room, planning colors and fabrics and furniture, laughing.

He had never loved her more.

"The nursery will be blue, the kitchen yellow, like sunshine, and we'll fill the house with roses. Can we plant roses, Anthony?"

"I thought you might say that."

"Is that a yes or a no?"

"Wait and see."

Annie pulled off her hard hat and tucked a stray curl behind her left ear.

"Does that mean you have a surprise for me, Anthony?"

"It wouldn't be a surprise if I told you."

"Oh! You!" She stalked around for all of two seconds, then her impatience turned to song as she toured her house once more, this time at a more sedate pace, planning and dreaming. He could follow her progress by a trail of off-key notes. Anthony smiled. Annie was singing their song: "It Had To Be You."

The surprise arrived early on Saturday morning, a delivery truck filled with roses, climbers and hybrids and rugosas, pink and white and red so dark, it looked like blood. There was even a rare blue rose in the lot.

So much beauty made Annie cry. Instead of being alarmed, Anthony understood. Kneeling in the dirt, he kissed her hand.

"Sometimes beauty makes me cry too." She noticed a telltale moisture in his eyes.

"We'll plant the blue rose right there, right where you're kneeling."

He got the shovel and lifted the first spade of dirt.

"It's my turn," she said.

He knew her too well to protest. Instead he wrapped his arms around her from behind and helped her ram the shovel into the earth.

She leaned against him, sighing. "Did I ever tell you how much I love you?"

He kissed the top of her hair. "Not since this morning."

Annie closed her eyes for a second, inhaling the scent of him, fresh, masculine, a combination of sea wind and summer sun and virile male. And while she had her eyes shut she said a prayer of thanksgiving that she had this summer in Fairhope with Anthony.

It hadn't been without a struggle, though.

Her mother had been aghast when Annie had revealed her plans.

"You are not going to spend the summer with a man?" she'd said.

"Not just any man, Mother. Anthony Chance."

Laura Ellen Harris worried the pearls at the neck of her yellow lawn dress. Beautiful, elegant, timid, and sheltered by her late husband's money, she seldom had the courage or the spirit to defy her headstrong daughter.

"Well, I know he's famous and all." She cut her eyes to the portrait of her daughter he'd presented Annie as an engagement present. "But how am I going to explain you spending the entire summer with him to my friends? New Orleans may be sophisticated, darling, but even a Harris is not immune to criticism when morals are involved."

"New Orleans society be hanged. I don't give a fig for convention."

"Well, I know that, dear."

Her mother had looked so lost and uncertain that Annie gathered her close the way she might a weeping child.

"Nobody has to know I'm with Anthony. Just tell them I'm supervising my first big job."

"Do you think they'll believe me?"

"Your friends are too polite not to believe you, Mother."

Remembering, she watched Anthony set their first rosebush into the hole they'd dug. And when he had finished, he kissed her on the cheek, sedate and whisper-soft. It might as well have been filled with sizzling desire judging by Annie's reaction.

Anthony chuckled. "This calls for a celebration."

"I couldn't agree with you more."

And they'd celebrated right there beside the newly planted bush. With the fragrance of rose perfuming the air and the soft sea breezes caressing their skin, they'd made slow, sweet love till hunger drove them to delve into the picnic basket they'd brought to the house site.

"You realize we still have eighteen rosebushes to plant?" Leaning toward him, she licked a bit of fried chicken crust off the corner of his lip.

"Are you lobbying for another celebration?"

"Always."

By the end of summer, the house was complete. Annie returned to New Orleans and to her studies, and Anthony moved back into his apartment in the French Quarter to be near her.

Every chance they got they browsed in antique shops and furniture stores and fabric shops, selecting items for their house and shipping them to Fairhope, where Anthony's cousin Waylon arranged them, as instructed.

By early December the house was furnished, everything except the bed. Though neither of them could describe what they wanted, they agreed they'd know it when they saw it.

"If we don't find the bed before June, does that mean the wedding's off?" she teased.

"Come June, I'm marrying you, with or without the bed."

The day was balmy, the hybrid camellia Fragrant Pink perfumed the air, and the lovers could hear the murmur of the river as they entered the antique shop. And there it was. The bed. *Their* bed.

They spotted it at the same time.

"It's rosewood," he said.

"It's perfect," she said.

"Look at that workmanship."

"I can't believe it. Carved roses."

They looked at each other, and a secret smile passed between them. An officious-looking proprietor left his vigil beside his desk and headed in their direction.

"It looks expensive," she whispered. "How much do you think it will cost?"

"Don't give the cost another thought. The pleasure will far outweigh the price."

The smell of his pomade preceded the shop owner by a good two feet.

"May I help you?" When he spoke his eyebrows disappeared into his heavily greased hair.

"We'll take this bed," Anthony said.

His eyebrows did a disappearing act once more. "We have some other very nice beds. Might I suggest you look at the Louis XIV before you buy."

"No, thank you. We want this bed."

"Very well, sir."

A Brahms cello sonata played in the background while he wrote the ticket. Annie hummed along softly, her eyes and cheeks aglow. Suddenly Anthony was filled with foreboding. He had an urge to toss her over his shoulder, race to the river, take the next freighter going south, and never look back.

It was on the tip of his tongue to say, "Annie, marry me . . . now," when the music was interrupted by an urgent announcement.

"Pearl Harbor has been bombed! I repeat, Pearl Harbor has been bombed!"

Annie turned as white as the dress she was wearing. He squeezed her hand.

"Anthony, let's get married. Now. Today."

They could do it, then sail away to the tropics, where he could paint and she could run along the beaches barefoot, wearing wild roses in her hair. With every fiber in his being he yearned to do her bidding. Theirs would be an idyllic life, full of sunshine and love and laughter. They could find a small island, build another house, start a family far away from the horrors of war.

The set crackled, and through the static the radio announcer told the details of the bombings. American ships had been sunk. Americans killed. America was in the war, whether she wanted to be or not.

Anthony didn't consider himself brave or patriotic, but he couldn't desert his country, *wouldn't* desert his country. Nor could he leave Annie a war bride, watching at the window for a soldier who might never come home.

He bent down and kissed the top of her head. "I have a better idea. Let's celebrate the purchase of our wedding bed."

Back in his apartment with the sun coming through the French windows and making patterns on their skin, he plunged into sweet, familiar territory. For a few blissful hours, Anthony and his beloved kept the world at bay.

TWELVE

The day Annie had been dreading finally came. It was mid-April, a gray rainy day appropriate for bad news. Standing at her bedroom window, the ruffled lace curtains of her childhood clenched into a ball in her right hand, she watched Anthony stride down the avenue of live oaks that led to her house in the Garden District. It hadn't been named that for nothing. Periodically he disappeared from view behind the long flower-bedecked arms of azaleas and the trailing yellow forsythia and the lush branches of sweet olive, starred with tiny fragrant white blossoms.

He rang the doorbell once. For a moment she thought of pretending she wasn't home. Later she could explain that she hadn't waited for him that Saturday as usual, that she'd driven over to Baton Rouge with her mother.

But she couldn't lie to him. She never had, and she wasn't about to start now.

She descended the staircase slowly, letting her fingers trail along the satiny mahogany. When she finally opened the door, she could see the pain in his eyes.

"Won't you come in? I've made tea."

She stood at a decorous distance, pronouncing all this carefully, as if formal manners would somehow change things, as if the small space between them could somehow soften the blow.

"Annie . . ."

"Please." She held up her hand. "I'll get the tea."

"I'll help you."

"No. Wait in the parlor." She lifted her eyes to his. "Please, Anthony."

In the kitchen safe from view she leaned over the sink, dry heaving. On the windowsill a mockingbird trilled, imitating the flashier, better-loved cardinal. Annie shook her fist at him.

"How dare you sing today. There's a war on, don't you know that?"

Without warning everything blurred—the mockingbird, the windowsill, the trees outside the window, the blue sky beyond. It wasn't until Anthony came up and softly turned her into his arms that she realized fat tears were pouring down her cheeks.

He kissed them away one by one, and she leaned into him, sighing.

"Don't go," she wanted to say, but she couldn't bring herself to be so selfish in the face of all the patriotic fervor, the sacrifice, and the acts of heroism told daily on the radio broadcasts.

"I've packed your bag," Anthony said.

Annie saw it sitting in the door, her coat draped over the top.

"I've come to take you away for a few days," he added.

He didn't have to add "to say farewell." Annie knew. She squeezed his hand, then went to the small desk in the corner of the kitchen and wrote a note to her mother.

"Anthony has enlisted. We're going to spend his last few days together. I'll see you soon. Love, Charlotte Ann."

When she turned back to him she was smiling. There would be no more tears. Charlotte Ann Harris planned to send her man off to war with a smile, and with all her love.

She never asked where he was taking her. Anthony loved that quality in his Annie. She trusted him absolutely. There was only one place he wanted to go, one place he wanted to remember: the house they had built together on the bay, the house she had designed, the house where they'd planted roses that would be in full bloom for their wedding day. Not June of '42. There was no telling where he would be in June of '42.

But someday. Somehow. Some June.

It was late afternoon when they arrived in Fairhope, laden with food and bedding.

"Let's have a picnic on the beach," she said.

"Wind's picking up. You'll get cold."

"You'll keep me warm."

They ate chicken she'd fried and potato salad he'd tossed and gingerbread boys with crooked bodies they'd both struggled to prepare.

Sprawled on a blanket with the picnic basket between them, they watched the sun go down.

"You know why I'm marrying you, don't you?" he teased.

"Absolutely. I'm a fabulous singer." To demonstrate she chortled a rollicking rendition of "The Lady's In Love With You," half a tone flatter than usual.

Anthony clapped his hands. "That, too, of course." He lifted another piece of chicken from the basket and savored a big bite. "But this"—he waved the drumstick at her—"this is the real reason I popped the question."

"Oh yeah?" Eyes gleaming, she stalked him. When she was even with him, she planted one foot on his chest and one hand on her hip.

"Annie, what are you doing?"

"I thought I'd give you another reason." She drew a circle on his chest with the toe of her shoe. "Or maybe two." Doing a delicate balancing act, she dragged her shoe downward until it was resting lightly on his groin.

"Be careful there. That's my family you're tinkering with."

"Mine too." She began a slow, erotic massage.

"Just so you know." His voice hoarse with passion, he made a move to pull her down, but she pressed lightly with the toe of her shoe.

"This is my show, Anthony Chance. Are you trying to steal my thunder?"

"I had something else in mind."

In the deepening shadows he could see her soft smile.

"If it's my heart you're talking about, you've already stolen that," she whispered.

"It's your heart . . . and more."

She stepped back and began to unfasten the tiny buttons on her bodice. Anthony folded his hands behind his head to watch. He knew what Annie was doing. She wasn't merely seducing him, wasn't simply undressing for the purpose of making love. She was creating magic that he would carry with him into war, a romantic moment that would burn into his mind like a comet so that when the horrors threatened to overwhelm him, he would remember, and the strength and beauty and power of the memory would bring him home again.

The moon came up, a disk of silver that laid its iridescent path on the water, and the stars lit slowly, one by one, like tiny fireflies filling the sky.

Annie cast her shirt to the ground, then spread her arms upward to rid herself of her camisole. Bare-breasted, she stood before him, stars caught in her hair, her skin gleaming like pearls.

Anthony thanked God for the evening shadows that hid his tears. Later that night, when she was fast asleep, he would sketch this memory of her, tuck it into his knapsack and take it wherever fate sent him.

Bending over him, the fragrance of roses wafting from her long hair, her nipples lightly brushing his lips, she unbuttoned his shirt. Breathless, Anthony waited, and memorized.

Her hair slid over one shoulder as she dipped downward and wet the indentation at the base of his throat with her tongue. The urge to take her then was so powerful, he had to suppress a deep groan, but this was her show, her moment. By a supreme act of willpower, he lay still on the blanket.

Her lips were roses touching his, lush and dewy and sweet. She lingered there, savoring him, letting him savor her, and the moon tracked across the sky.

When he was near the point of explosion, she rose and slid her skirt and petticoat down her hips. The evening had grown cool, but Annie didn't wrap her arms around herself to keep warm. Instead she lifted her arms and stood before him like some night-loving, cold-immune goddess.

"Come, my love," she whispered, beckoning.

He didn't question, but stood and shucked off the clothes that restricted him. She led him to the sea. Water lapped against their ankles, then their knees, and in the luminescence created by reflections of moon and stars in the bay he could see the goose bumps that dotted her fine skin.

"I've always wanted to swim naked with you in the bay in the moonlight," she whispered.

He caught her in his arms and waded waist-deep, holding her tightly against the warmth of his chest, high above the waves.

"And what else, my love?"

"This." She kissed him again, a deep kiss that went

Only Yesterday

into eternity. "And this." In one smooth move she was out of his arms and swimming strongly away, diving and resurfacing, a mermaid frolicking in the moonlight, her skin cast silver by the stars.

He swam after her, meeting her in a wave that sprayed their faces with foam. She came to him then, arms and legs open. Wrapped tightly together, they rode the waves and each other, and afterward they strolled along the beach, Annie wearing her white dress without camisole and petticoats and Anthony with his arms wrapped around her.

Speaking softly lest they disturb the enchantment, they talked until they were hoarse, talked of everything from architecture to art, from religion to politics, from building houses to making babies. But neither of them mentioned war.

They slept curled tightly together in a twin bed in their guest room. Down the hall the rosewood bed stood in lonely splendor, draped with sheets, awaiting its grand unveiling on their wedding night.

The days and nights blended, one so like the other in joy that Annie couldn't have told whether it was Tuesday or Saturday. But the morning she woke to find Anthony standing at the window, she knew the time had come to say good-bye. There was resolve in every line of his body, from the stiff angle of his neck to the unyielding posture of his back.

Her heart lurched, and she pressed her hand over her mouth to keep from crying out.

Anthony turned from the window, and she forced a smile.

"Shall I start the coffee?" she said, hoping he'd grin and climb back into bed and gather her close and make love to her until the sun was over the top of the magnolia, as he had on so many mornings.

He shook his head. "It's already made. I was waiting for you to wake up." The springs squeaked as he sat beside her. Cupping her face, he gazed deeply at her, then pressed a sweet, lingering kiss on her lips.

The springs creaked once more. "Wait right here. I'm serving you breakfast in bed today."

He was at the door before she could trust herself to speak.

"Shall I pack?"

"Yes."

That was all he said. And then he was gone.

Naked, she flung clothes into her bag, neither knowing nor caring whether they wrinkled. Then she brushed her hair. Her hands shook so badly, she dropped her silver-handled brush three times.

When she heard his footsteps on the stairs, she leaped back into bed, a smile on her face.

"That was fast," she said. "Can I interest you in a job as my butler?"

"Your butler . . ." He kissed her cheek. "Your footman . . ." He kissed her nose. "Your slave." He kissed her mouth. "Forever and always, Annie."

He set the tray on the bed, food in artistic array and a single paper rose resting on the white linen napkin.

Then he sat solemnly beside her and watched her eat until every morsel was gone.

"Do I get dessert?" she asked, her smile full of wicked whimsy.

"You do. But first, this." From his knapsack he took the Felix the Cat clock, fully wound, tail wagging and pop eyes rolling. It was a happy clock, just the kind of thing Anthony would choose.

"To mark the time until we meet again," he said, and then he folded her in his arms and held her close to his heart.

That summer Annie and her mother moved into the house on the bay to await Anthony's return.

"But why Fairhope, Charlotte Ann? Why can't we wait out the war here in New Orleans?" Her mother's protests had been mild, considering what Annie wanted her to do, pull up roots and leave her home and her friends behind.

"Because I want Anthony to picture me in that house, waiting for him. It's a show of faith and confidence, Mother. If he knows I'm there waiting for him where we'll build our life and our family, he'll come home. I just know he will."

And in June instead of walking down the aisle in white as she'd planned, Charlotte Ann Harris took her mother to Fairhope to wait for the war to be over.

Daily she wrote to Anthony.

"August 8, 1942. My darling, I know from the news that the first Allied offensive in the Pacific War began yesterday when the Marines went ashore at Guadalcanal. I feel better knowing you're in the sky. When you're flying up there, touch the stars, my love, and know that I wait for you at home. All my love, Annie."

Summer turned to fall, and except for the calendar Annie didn't know the difference. The air was stifling, and she spent most of her days barefoot, curled on a blanket under the magnolia tree reading Anthony's letters, and writing.

"September 30, 1942. My dearest love, It does my heart good to know that you're on a brand-new cruiser and that furthermore it's full of Southern rebels. Nobody can give 'em hell the way a rebel can. I'm counting the minutes until you come home, with the help of Felix the Cat, of course. Forever and always, Annie."

She mailed his Christmas package in November in the hopes it would reach him in time.

"Let's not bother with a tree this year," her mother said, but Annie insisted.

"It'll keep our spirits up," she said.

The days became weeks, the weeks became months, and Annie haunted the mailbox. Every time a letter arrived, she breathed a sigh of relief.

On the other side of the world, Anthony Chance lived up to his name. He took chances in his fighter plane that no other pilot would dare. He made light of his exploits to Annie, knowing she would worry, never dreaming she'd hear of them anyway through a series of articles written by a war correspondent.

"My darling Annie," he wrote to her. "In a few hours I go up for the last time before I ship out for home. Always, I think of you waiting there for me, and the thought gives me courage. The stars are out tonight, almost as bright as they were that evening we went swimming in the bay. I close my eyes and see you there with stars in your hair. I can't wait to touch you, to hold you, to make love to you. Count the hours, my love, dust the rosewood bed. I'm coming home. Always, Anthony."

His plane was a dark shadow on the deck of the cruiser. Anthony climbed into the cockpit and gave the thumbs-up signal, then touched the small sketch of Annie he always kept in his breast pocket.

As the plane climbed into the star-studded heavens he felt as if he were flying straight toward the face of God. His targets were below, visible by the light of the star shells fired by the *Montpelier*.

Anthony flew in low, target locked in. There was an explosion, a burst of fire along his right wing, and then a plume of smoke. Stars ricocheted past the cockpit as his plane rocked and bucked.

He fought for control, refusing to believe what had happened. Tomorrow he was shipping out for home. He couldn't be hit.

"No!" His defiant yell was lost in the screaming of the plane as it spiraled downward. Anthony touched the picture of Annie over his heart, then clenched his teeth against the dizzying speed of his descent and tried to force his plane back into a climb. A huge expanse of gunmetal gray came rapidly toward him, the Pacific, cold and forbidding in the dark.

Anthony clung to consciousness, registering events in bits and pieces. Another burst of flame. Blinding light. Metal ripping. Searing pain. Cold. Wet. Tunnel. Spiraling.

"Annie!" *I'll come for you, Annie. I'll find a way.*

Darkness, soft and peaceful.

And then the light.

The officer who stood in her doorway was young and ill at ease. Annie knew she ought to try and make him feel more comfortable—it was the way of Southern hospitality—but she couldn't think how, couldn't think of anything except the knapsack he was holding.

"His possessions." The officer's name was James, Lieutenant James. "He wanted you to have them . . ." Lieutenant James stuttered to a halt. ". . . in case anything happened to him."

Annie recognized the knapsack. She'd seen it hundreds of times, on the floor of her closet, under her bed, behind Anthony's art supplies, in the trunk of his car. She clasped her hands tightly together, refusing to accept it.

"Anthony's coming home." Her face was tight, her smile exaggerated, her skin hot.

"His plane went down in the Pacific."

"No." She raised a hand to stop him.

"He was a hero, Miss Harris. He died for his country."

"NOOO!"

"I'm sorry, Miss Harris. If there's anything I can do for you . . ." His voice trailed off, and finally Lieutenant James set the knapsack on the front porch. His footsteps sounded like cannon fire on the porch floor. At the steps he paused, then turned back to her.

"If it makes you feel any better, Miss Harris, he was a damned fine soldier and a gentleman."

Her face was frozen, her voice locked, her feet nailed down.

The day was beautiful in the sun, as bright as the wings of a bluebird. She and Anthony would go sailing when he got home. They would picnic on the beach, then when the sun went down and the moon came up, they'd swim naked with nothing but the stars to keep them company . . . when Anthony got home.

She would put on her white dress and walk down the aisle, and he would be waiting for her at the altar, when he got home. Anthony would lift her off her feet and twirl her around when he got home. He would . . .

Pain knocked her to her knees. She buried her face in his knapsack, sobbing. Anthony was not coming home. He would never come home.

Annie grabbed the knapsack and hurled it as far as she could. "You promised," she screamed. "You promised."

Blinded by tears, she raced into the house.

"Charlotte Ann," her mother called, but Annie kept on going.

The clock was sitting on her bedside table, marking time until they would meet again.

"You said you would come for me. You promised."

Her hand closed over the cold plastic clock, and she collapsed onto the bed, hugging it close.

Outside a sudden summer storm burst over the land, and the room was suddenly bright with lightning.

"Charlotte Ann?" Her mother's voice was faint and far away.

Another burst of brilliant light. Then she was sucked into a funnel of darkness.

"Anthony . . . Anthony . . ."

THIRTEEN

The candle burned low, the air shimmered with electrical currents, and the clock lay on its side on the attic floor, split in half.

Ann pressed her hands to her temples, trying to ease the pressure. Images crowded in on her, and raw emotions threatened her sanity. The images were vague, like something she might have dreamed long ago, and yet they were far more compelling than dream memories.

Had they traveled through time, as Colt had suggested? Was he Anthony Chance? Was she Charlotte Ann Harris?

What was the truth? And would she ever know?

"The letters," she said suddenly.

"They're all in the trunk."

"Not Anthony's letters to my grandmother." She raced to the trunk. "Her letters to him."

She knelt and scrambled frantically through the

contents of the trunk. There were Anthony's letters to Charlotte Ann, a silk shawl, a box of photographs, a paper rose, a diamond ring, a silk dressing gown, a pair of satin mules, and in the bottom a wedding gown, wrapped in blue tissue paper.

But no letters from Charlotte Ann Harris to Anthony Chance.

Flushed, she looked at Colt. "They're not here. Her letters are not here."

Colt knelt beside her and chafed her hands as if she were a shock victim he'd recently pulled from a burning fire. Which wasn't far from the truth.

"It's all right, Annie," Colt said. "Everything's going to be all right."

He handed her a mug of coffee. "Drink this. It's cold, but the jolt of caffeine is just what you need."

Her mind was whirling like a merry-go-round, and while she sipped she tried to make sense of the strange events.

"Better?" Colt said.

"Better." She managed a smile. "Thank you."

"My pleasure."

"I don't know why. I've been a real witch."

"Never a dull moment with you, Annie."

She didn't protest about the name this time. Instead she concentrated on gaining control of herself.

When she'd finished the coffee, Colt set the mug aside, then settled on the floor beside her, close but not touching. Just looking at him was temptation enough. She was grateful for small favors.

Only Yesterday

"How did you know about your grandmother's letters?"

How did she? They weren't in the trunk. She couldn't have seen them. Before the hurricane she hadn't known about the affair with Anthony Chance, so nobody in the family would have mentioned them.

But she remembered them so clearly. The way Charlotte Ann described waiting in the house Anthony had built, the terms of endearment she used, the gut-deep fear that she would lose the love of her life.

Ann had a floating sensation, as if her spirit were circling somewhere in another realm and her body had been left behind on the attic floor.

"Don't you know, Annie?" Colt took her hands and placed a tender kiss in her palms. "We're the lovers in those letters. Anthony Chance finally kept his word to his Annie."

What he said felt so right, so perfect. Their instant attraction, their striking likeness to the lovers, the way Colt used Anthony's exact phrases, the compelling sense of déjà vu—it all made sense in light of what Colt was saying.

And yet, believing him meant taking a giant leap of faith in a realm as misunderstood as it was mystical. It meant discounting such things as logic and common sense and carefully laid plans.

And it meant breaking Rob's heart.

"I don't believe you," she said.

"Didn't you learn anything when you went back the second time?"

"I didn't go back in time. I had a small blackout spell, that's all."

"How do you explain your knowledge of your grandmother's letters?"

"Logic. Anthony wrote to her. She must have written back."

Colt plucked the paper rose from the trunk.

"Remember this?"

Flashes. Images. The breakfast tray, the smell of the new house, the wrenching pain of good-bye. Where did it all come from? What was happening to her?

She shook her head, unwilling to admit what she was seeing, feeling.

"Yes," she said. "I remember. When I searched the trunk I found the rose tucked between the folds of my grandmother's silk dressing gown."

Was that disappointment she saw on his face? Disapproval? Heartbreak? She couldn't bear to look.

The attic suddenly felt small and stifling.

"How soon do you think we can leave?" she said.

"As soon as it's safe."

"What's your best estimate?"

"I'm no magician, Annie . . . merely a reincarnation."

"Don't say that!"

In New York she'd always been in command, no matter what the situation. Nosy landlords, bossy art gallery owners, snobbish clients, lover's spats—she was equal to them all. And yet storm-trapped in the attic with one handsome man, she couldn't seem to control anything, least of all her feelings.

More than anything in the world she wanted to touch Colt, merely touch him. And it was broad daylight. What would happen when it got dark?

Without warning the tears started. She tried to dash them away with the back of her hand, but they kept coming.

"I'm sorry. I'm really not a crybaby. I don't know what's the matter with me."

Colt couldn't bear her tears. Furthermore, he couldn't bear to be the cause of her tears.

"There now." He took her in his arms. "Go ahead and cry. After the last few days you deserve a good cry."

"You think so?" Her smile was watery.

"Indeed, I do."

"I hope you have a handkerchief handy."

"If we run out of linen, you can use the tail of my shirt."

She hiccuped once, then boo-hooed in earnest. He patted her shoulder and smoothed her hair and murmured words of comfort and generally enjoyed the hell out of the moment, which would have made absolutely no sense to him if it hadn't been for his recent experience.

If anyone had told him two weeks before that he'd be claiming the identity of a man who died in a plane crash in World War II, he'd have said they were crazy. But in light of his incredible journey back through time, he now understood things that had made no sense to him. For instance, the way he dated then discarded women, like a man constantly searching.

He had been, of course. Searching for Annie. And now that he'd found her, he'd be damned if he was going to let her go.

But neither would he push. He was a patient man. He could wait a few more weeks, even months. After all, he'd already waited more than fifty years.

Charlotte Ann Harris had loved Anthony Chance. But that was another time. The trick was to make Charlotte Ann Debeau love Colt Butler, a man she knew very little about.

He pulled a handkerchief out of the pocket of the jeans he'd been wearing and handed it to her.

"Thanks." She wiped her face and blew her nose. "I must be a mess."

"You are, but a gorgeous mess."

"My nose gets red when I cry. Like Rudolph's."

"Like a rose."

She laughed. He loved that about her, that she could go from tears to laughter in a heartbeat.

"You're a hard man not to like, Colt Butler."

"I'm a hard man."

"You'll be happy to know, I've decided not to take offense at anything else you say. After all, you risked your life for me."

"Shoot. Where's the fun in being a pain in the butt if I can't get a rise out of you."

He'd made her smile again. That was progress.

"No more talk of the past," he said.

"Agreed." Relief flooded her face.

"What do you say we share another pastry and then head to bed?"

She glanced toward the pallet they'd shared, and her cheeks turned pink. "I'm not all that sleepy," she said, suppressing a yawn.

"I am." He dragged the chaise longue out of the dusty corner of the attic and spread the best of the covers over it. "Miss Ann Debeau, your bed."

"What about you?"

"For the duration of our stay, I'm claiming the floor." A stubborn look crossed her face. "No argument," he added.

"Okay. No argument."

She settled onto the chaise and pulled the covers up. Colt blew out the candle, then wrapped himself in the patchwork quilt.

"Good night, Annie."

" 'Night, Colt."

A single star lit the attic window, as bright as a promise.

FOURTEEN

The minute Ann woke up she sensed a change. Dust swirled and danced in the patches of sun that shone through the window. She turned her head slowly and saw Colt at the window, resignation in every line of his body.

Ann lay still under the covers watching him, her heart in such tumult, she thought she was going to split in half. Something alerted him—a sigh, a breath, a thought.

"Annie?" He pivoted and smiled at her, but it was not his usual carefree grin. "You're awake."

"Yes." She threw back the covers. "I see the sun's out."

Barefoot, she joined him at the window. His arm slid around her, and she leaned against his shoulder as naturally as a willow bends into the wind. His boat, lashed to the magnolia tree, drifted the length of its rope, swaying gently. The angry force of the waves had carried away all the debris, and nothing stood between them and the boat except a shining expanse of water.

"I'll swim out and get the boat," he said. She nodded, too full of emotion to speak. "Get whatever you want to take with you. I'll get as close to the window as possible."

"It's over, then."

He cupped her face. "It's not over, Annie. It will never be over between us."

He kissed her softly, then with a wink and a smile he climbed out the window.

"Be careful," she called after him, then watched until he was safely in the boat.

The only thing she took besides her toiletries was her Felix the Cat clock. Then touching the dried roses Colt had given her, she made a promise. "I'll be back for you, later."

A beam of sunlight illuminated her grandmother's portrait as Ann climbed out the window.

News of the dramatic rescue reached the press, and reporters were waiting for them. Bulbs flashed and microphones were stuck into their faces as Colt helped Ann from the little boat.

The reporters shouted a barrage of questions: "Miss Debeau? What was it like being stranded in Windchime House? How long were you there? How did you manage for three days? What are your plans now?"

She answered all their questions as briefly as possible, and then they turned their attention to Colt.

"Mr. Butler, what made you risk your life for Miss Debeau?"

Colt looked at her, and she saw the answer in his eyes.

"In any rescue operation, there's always risk," he told reporters, his face giving away nothing.

"Yes, but this one was particularly risky." The woman from the *Times Picayune* pushed her way forward. "What made you do it?"

"Miss Debeau has been through a terrible ordeal. I'm sure you'll understand if we cut this interview short."

Colt put his arm around her and whisked her away.

"Thanks," she whispered.

"No problem." He hustled her into his car.

"Where are you taking me?"

"My place. You'll have more privacy there than at a motel."

His place, as he so modestly called it, was an enormous polo ranch on Highway 32 east of Point Clear. In spite of the damage from high winds and torrential rains, the estate was lush and inviting, peaceful in a way that only country estates can be with acres of woods and sparkling lakes and rolling meadows as far as the eye could see.

Horses with shining coats grazed in fields and frolicked in the paddocks. Birdsong and the perfume of summer flowers filled the air as if all of nature celebrated the end of the storm and the beginning of a season of promise.

An old man who looked like a cross between a Santa Claus and a grizzly bear greeted them at the front door.

"Annie, meet Uncle Pete."

Colt's uncle took both her hands and kissed her warmly on the cheek. "You're Charlotte Ann's granddaughter," he said. "There's no mistaking the resemblance."

"You knew her?"

"Your granddaddy was a friend of mine. They boarded horses just down the road. He used to bring Charlotte Ann out here to ride."

"I barely knew my granddaddy, and didn't know my grandmother at all. Perhaps you can tell me more about them."

"Over chicken soup. You're skinny as a rail."

Pete led the way to the kitchen, and Colt winked at Annie.

"Don't let him intimidate you, Annie. He's spent thirty years trying to whip me into shape."

Pete set two heaping bowls of soup on the table. "You'd still benefit from my advice, if only you'd listen." He sat beside Annie and nursed a big cup of coffee. "Colt never listens to a thing anybody says. He's always marched to his own drummer."

"I'm sure Annie doesn't want to hear about me. Why don't you tell her more about her grandparents."

On the contrary, Ann wanted very much to hear

more about the man who had climbed through the attic window and stolen her heart, but she didn't tell him that. As long as she wore Rob's ring, she had no right to say such things.

And even if she didn't wear his ring, she still had no right to assume a personal role in Colt's life, simply because of what had happened in the attic. Until she could sort through those events, she was going to proceed with caution.

"This soup is delicious," she said.

"Thanks. I made it from scratch. I'm a darned good cook, if I do say so myself." His gaze slid from Ann to Colt, then back again. "I taught Colt everything I know about cooking."

Ann laughed. "I thought his talents didn't extend beyond cold toaster pastries."

"You haven't seen half his talents yet." Ann nearly choked on her soup. "Wait till you see him ride. Do you like polo?"

"Pete . . ."

Colt's good-natured warning brought Pete back around to the subject of Ann's grandparents.

"Let me see, now . . . I knew Richard for many years. Everybody did. He was the postmaster of Fairhope."

"Is that how he met my grandmother?"

"Yep. During the war she was all the time going to pick up letters, and when the letters stopped, Richard went a-calling, to see what was wrong. Your granddaddy was like that. A fine, caring man. He worshiped the ground Charlotte Ann walked on."

Only Yesterday

Enthralled, Ann leaned across the table, devouring every word. Her parents had been interested only in their own lives, and Aunt Gilly hadn't been one to pass on oral family history. Not that Ann would have listened. Life occurred in stages, beginning with the self-centered stage that lasted from childhood through early adolescence. After that came the striving stage when getting through college and starting a career were all that mattered.

Ann believed that everything happened in its own time. And now was the time for family history.

Pete talked until she began to nod off.

Colt took her gently by the hand. "Say good night, Uncle Pete. Annie's going to bed."

"Are you always this bossy?" she asked on the upstairs landing.

"It's one of my many talents." His grin was wicked. "You want to see my others?"

"I'm too tired to rise to the bait."

He opened the door to a spacious bedroom filled with antiques. Inside, he kissed her on the forehead.

"That bed looks so inviting," she said.

"Yes, it does."

Suddenly self-conscious, she realized that their thoughts were straying in the same direction. Her theory about attraction being based on the element of danger vanished in a sigh.

"Take off your clothes, Annie."

"What?"

"I'm going to wash them." Colt handed her a robe hanging on the peg behind the door. "You can wear this. And I think you'll find an old T-shirt of mine in the top drawer over there." He nodded toward a cherry highboy.

"Thank you, Colt." She stepped back a discreet distance. "You've been more than kind."

He kissed her hand. "You're more than welcome, Annie, my love."

Everything that had been between them in the attic burst into full flower, and she was tempted right then and there to shed her clothes and lead him to the big double bed. So very tempted.

Unconsciously she twisted the ring on her finger.

"If I can get a plane out, I'll leave tomorrow."

He tilted her chin upward with the tips of his fingers. "Is that what you want to do?"

"It's what I have to do."

They stood together at the airport. Beyond the Jetway the plane waited that would take her to New York. A lassitude overtook her, and Ann wanted nothing more than to sit in a quiet corner and not move for the next few days.

"Annie, look at me." She did, and what she saw in his eyes stole her breath. "This is not good-bye."

"I have to go back, Colt."

"You'll return."

As quickly as it had come the lassitude vanished, and in its place was a spitfire who had gone through hell and back and who had come out fighting.

"How do you know that? Just because we both

dreamed the same dream doesn't mean we're connected."

He tucked her hair behind her left ear. "We did dream the same dream, Annie. We still do."

The announcement came over the loudspeaker. "Last call for Flight 365 to LaGuardia."

"When the floodwaters recede, you'll be back to Windchime House to claim what's yours . . . and I'll claim what's mine."

He kissed her then, a long, lingering kiss that made her heart lurch and her toes curl under. She turned quickly from him so he wouldn't see her tears.

And when the plane lifted toward New York, she could see him still, a tiny speck, shading his eyes for one last glimpse.

FIFTEEN

Rob was waiting for Ann at the airport. She felt like a traitor as she walked into his arms.

"Ann, my God. I can't believe you're finally home."

"I can't believe it, either."

He bent down, and she turned her face slightly to the left so that his kiss landed on her cheek.

"It's good to be back, Rob."

Why was it that everything she said felt like a lie? In many ways she was glad to be back—glad to be out of danger, glad to be returning to her studio, to her work.

He gathered her bags and hustled her into a limo. Though he could well afford it, it wasn't like him to be so extravagant.

"I decided to give you the royal treatment. Hurricane victim returns, triumphant. Reunited at last with her lover."

Ann's smile vanished. Memories bombarded her,

flashing between past and present—a sunlit bed in the French Quarter, the wedding gown in a dusty trunk in the attic, Colt sleeping with one arm thrown over his head, Colt taking them safely from the flooded attic, Colt seeing her off at the airport in Pensacola.

Ann leaned her head against the soft leather seat and closed her eyes.

"Tired?" Rob said.

"Very."

He patted her hand. "Don't worry, darling. I'll take care of you."

She kept her eyes closed. The last thing in the world she wanted was Rob "taking care of her" and all that statement implied.

"That's very sweet of you, Rob, but I would be terrible company this evening. All I want to do is go back to my apartment, take a bath, and crawl into bed."

He couldn't hide his irritation. "I had planned a lovely dinner at Carmine's. I thought you'd want some good Italian cooking after that deep South diet. What is it? Redeye gravy and biscuits?"

"Not everybody eats that way. Believe it or not, some people in the South are actually health conscious."

"Now, Ann. There's no need to get huffy. I was only teasing."

"Sorry, Rob. I guess I'm not in the mood for teasing."

She wasn't in the mood for anything, at least not with Rob. As the limousine whizzed through the streets of New York, she studied his profile. Handsome with a strong jaw and a Roman nose, the premature gray at his temples giving him a distinguished look, he was the kind of man that single women sought out at cocktail parties. Any woman would be happy to be in Ann's shoes.

Then why wasn't she happy?

She was too tired to ponder the reasons. Sighing, she turned her face back to the window.

Rob reached for her hand. Ann remembered another hand she'd held, a strong, suntanned hand belonging to a man who had the power to turn her inside out.

From the bag at her feet came the faint sound of ticking—Felix the Cat, Colt's gift to Annie, "to mark time until we meet again."

"We'll talk tomorrow," she told Rob.

The dinner bell clanged, echoing across the pasture to the edge of the woods where Colt stood. With a hammer in one hand and nails in the other, he lifted his head and listened.

He didn't need a bell to tell him it was dinnertime. His stomach was doing a good job of that. He held the wire in place and drove the nail home, then surveyed the length of fence. Bethany had done some damage to his ranch, mostly to fences and roofs, and he'd spent the morning making repairs.

The bell clanged again. Weary, Colt mounted Warrior and raced to the house. Pete was in the sunny kitchen dishing up red beans and rice.

Only Yesterday

"You look like hell," Pete said.

"I don't feel much better."

"It's no wonder. Out all hours helping folks clean up after Bethany, then running from can till can't getting this ranch back in shape. What're you trying to do? Kill yourself?"

"Just trying to get the job done, that's all."

And stay so busy he didn't have time to think. If he thought about Annie in New York with Rob, he'd drive himself crazy.

"There's more to it than that, and I suspect it has something to do with Windchime House and Ann Debeau," Pete said.

Across the kitchen table, Pete gave him an expectant look, but Colt didn't bite.

"Three days is a long time to be trapped in an attic with a beautiful woman."

There was another pregnant pause, but Colt kept eating his food.

"A lot can happen in three days," Pete said hopefully.

"Yep. A lot can happen."

In three days a man could learn that it was possible for a woman to get tangled up in his heart with a single look, that hearts intertwined could remain that way for a lifetime, and beyond.

For a while there was no sound in the kitchen except the scraping of forks against plates and a contented sigh as Pete dredged his corn bread through the remains of his dinner and took that last satisfying bite.

Hands crossed on his belly, Pete leaned back in his chair.

"When's she coming back?"

"She didn't say."

Pete left off prying for a while to give Colt what he called the "once-over." Though his eyes were rheumy with age, he had no trouble at all making Colt feel as if Pete were seeing right through him. And he had an uncanny knack for getting to the heart of the matter.

Ever since her plane had lifted toward New York, Colt had asked himself the same thing. When was she coming back? *Was* she coming back?

Pete refilled his coffee cup and looked beyond Colt to the darkening sky and the first star of evening that shone through the kitchen window.

"I never get tired of this view," he said.

"I feel the same way. A man could do worse than spend his life riding his land with the wind in his hair and a good horse beneath him."

Pete gave him a piercing look. "He could do better too."

Silent, Colt refilled his own coffee cup.

"Did I ever tell you about Erma Jean?" Pete had a horror of falling into the habit of repeating himself that plagued most people his age, and so the look he gave Colt was anxious and hopeful at the same time.

"No, you didn't."

"I thought not." Pete nodded, satisfied. "Erma Jean was the prettiest little thing in Alabama, blond hair and silvery eyes and silky skin. She put me in mind of a fine

Alberta peach. Met her at a barn dance. We fell in love at first sight."

"What happened?"

"She married another man and moved to Florida."

"Was it because of me?"

Colt had been a scared five-year-old when he'd come to live with his daddy's brother. Nightmares used to wake him up, and he'd sit up in bed, sweating and shaking, his mouth open but no sound coming out as he replayed the scene on the polo field when his daddy toppled off Spirit Dancer and his mother had run screaming onto the field, right in the path of thundering hooves.

Pete would reach out and tuck Colt close, then tell him stories about his daddy's childhood until he fell asleep.

"Had nothing to do with you," Pete said. "It was a long time before Caleb and Vivien died." He steepled his fingers, remembering. "I had too many things I wanted to do, too many horses to train, and I thought Erma Jean would wait forever. She didn't."

Colt didn't ask why Pete had never found anybody else. Now that he'd met Annie, he knew.

Pete lowered his busy eyebrows as he stared at Colt. "It gets mighty lonesome in a bed all by yourself."

How well Colt knew. A vision of Annie came to him, asleep on the chaise longue with one hand resting under her cheek. It had taken every ounce of willpower he possessed not to go to her and gather her in his arms.

"Yes, a man can get lonesome," Colt said, then picked up his hat and rammed it on his head.

"Where are you going?"

"Fairhope. The Crockers are going to need help."

And after the Crockers, the Gibbs, then after them the Rakestraws, and on and on until one fine day Colt would look up and Annie would be back in Windchime House, back where she belonged.

SIXTEEN

Surrounded by the tools of her trade—wheels, globs of clay, pots of glaze—Ann felt more at ease, more confident and not nearly as scared as she'd been the previous night as she lay in her bed and came to a decision about her future.

Barefoot, wearing jeans and a white shirt with the tail hanging out, she sat behind her potter's wheel turning a delicate vase while Rob perched on the edge of the sofa underneath the skylight.

"Do you have to do that?" he said, nodding toward the wet clay taking shape underneath her fingertips.

"Yes. I have to do this."

"I thought you wanted to talk."

"I do, but I feel more comfortable talking here in my studio."

"I don't know why we couldn't have had this conversation over dinner. I was thinking of the Vegetarian

Paradise in Chinatown. Or even in my apartment, where we could relax with the hot tub."

Still dressed in his suit and tie, he looked out of place in her cluttered studio and uncomfortable besides. But he didn't betray himself by so much as a blink of his eye. He didn't even loosen his tie.

Ann concentrated on a delicate maneuver on the wheel, then lifted her gaze to him.

"What I have to say is not easy, Rob."

"Look, I know you were tired when you came in last night. I understand. Believe me." He picked up a handblown blue glass ball from the coffee table and tested its weight, then set it back down. "I think you're still tired and overwrought, and whatever you have to say should wait until you've fully recovered from the trauma of what happened to you down South."

"I don't think I'll ever fully recover, Rob."

He left the sofa to squat beside her wheel, one hand on her knee.

"We'll get help for you, darling. There are some very good psychologists who specialize in these matters."

"I don't need a psychologist. I need time."

"I agree. Time will help, but a trained professional can make all the difference between full recovery and partial."

She cut off the wheel, wiped her hands on a towel, and covered his hand with both of hers.

"You are dear in so many ways."

He was intuitive enough to hear more than the compliment in her voice.

"Don't say anything else, Ann. Not yet. Give it some time."

"That's exactly what I plan to do."

Restless, uncertain, and more than a little scared, she left the wheel to pace her studio. Pottery pieces she'd created lined the shelves, and she paused to run her hands over them, taking courage from the graceful lines and the cool surfaces.

He was a powerful presence behind her, a man whose arms had held her close at night, a man who had charmed her with stories of his childhood and earned her respect with the conscientious way he treated his clients, each case as if it were special.

Ann twisted the ring on her finger, wondering for the hundredth time if she were making a mistake. Rob caught her from behind and pulled her close, burying his face in her hair.

"God, I've missed you."

She waited for something to happen to her—anything—shivers, sparks, joy. But she felt nothing except a mild comfort.

"Let's go to your bedroom, Ann."

"No." She gently pulled herself free, then faced him with her chin up and her heart full of resolve. "There's no easy way to say this, Rob. All I know how to do is to be perfectly candid. I can't go on with our engagement."

She pulled off the ring and pressed it into his hand. He studied the large diamond, his jaw set.

He shoved the ring into his pocket. "What happened down there?"

"I don't like your tone or your implication."

"You didn't answer my question. You were holed up in that attic for three days with a man. Exactly how did you pass the time, Ann?"

"Am I under oath, Counselor?"

"Okay." He held up his hands. "Maybe I deserved that. But you have to admit that your actions coming right on the heels of that dramatic rescue add up to more than coincidence."

Ann dropped her face into her hands, suddenly tired of everything. She could feel his anger pulsing across the space that separated them.

"Nothing happened," she said, lifting her head. "Not what you're thinking."

His mouth grim, he waited. Ann tilted her chin upward a notch.

"We played chess and checkers and took turns checking on the water level outside our window. We ate cold pastries and canned Viennas and drank cold coffee."

Memories flooded her, and she took a shaky breath.

"That accounts for the daylight hours," he said.

Not quite, but the letters were too personal to share with Rob. And the old clock with its incredible magic.

"If you're asking whether we had sex, the answer is no. But not because I didn't want to." She tilted her face so she could look him squarely in the eye. "I wanted Colt Butler, Rob. I was engaged to you but I wanted another man, and that's why I didn't let you come to my bed last night and that's why I didn't sleep a wink and that's why I'm ending this engagement. It's not fair."

"To whom, Ann? To me or to him?"

"There are three people involved here, and an engagement that is not real and true is not fair to any of us."

"So now that the engagement doesn't stand in your way, you're going to him?"

"I can understand your bitterness . . ."

"You can't possibly understand." Rob raked his hand through his hair, a gesture she'd never seen him use. "I spend years working so I can make it to the top of the heap, hardly taking time to eat, let alone have a social life. Then I find the perfect woman, plan the perfect life . . . And suddenly this."

He made a slashing motion across his throat. "No, Ann, you don't understand."

He strode toward the door, anger echoing in every step he took.

"Rob, wait." She caught up to him, put her hand on his arm. "I didn't want it to end this way."

"You're the one who ended it, Ann." Some of the fight went out of him, and he leaned against the door. "What did you expect of me?"

"I really don't know. If it makes you feel any better, the answer is *no*. I'm not going back to Alabama. At least, not for a while."

"What will you do?"

"Work, recover, think."

He studied her, and for a moment his face softened. But the interlude was brief.

"I wish I could say, call me if you change your mind, but I can't. I don't believe in second chances, Ann."

"I do," she whispered, but he didn't hear her. He was already out the door.

Charlotte Ann and Anthony flashed into her mind, whirling in a slow, sweet tango of love.

Ann raced to the window and watched as Rob climbed into his car. Suddenly she thought of a dozen things she'd wanted to say to him—you're a good man, take care of yourself, someday you'll find a woman who will love you the way you deserve to be loved.

Ann left the window, wet her hands, and went to her wheel. The clay felt alive, and for a while she lost herself in her art. She knew who she was. Ann Debeau, Brooklyn, New York, twentieth century.

The stars spread across the sky, and a moon as big as Kansas peeped through Ann's window. Without warning she smelled jasmine, saw the intricate carvings on the iron balcony in New Orleans, heard Anthony's laughter, felt his hands on her breasts.

And she was torn in two.

The wheel wobbled, the piece tilted, and the delicate vase she'd been shaping turned into a heap of clay.

Ann leaned her head against the cold clay and cried.

There was activity at Windchime House. Colt braked his car, made a sharp turn, and raced up the driveway. Trucks with logos crowded the lawn, and

Only Yesterday

carpenters, plumbers, painters, and roofers swarmed over the house.

Parking beside a van with CROFT PLUMBING on the side in red letters, Colt went up the front porch steps. A man in green coveralls was coming out the door.

"I'm Colt Butler."

"I know who you are." The man spat a stream of tobacco over the railing. "Seen your picture in the paper."

"I see you're cleaning up the place."

"Yep."

Colt's insides were humming with excitement, but he knew better than to barrel up to Windchime House and start asking questions. That wasn't the way things were done down South. If you wanted to find out something, you had to take a roundabout approach.

He surveyed the work that had already been done on the front.

"It looks good," he said. "First class."

"Yep. Work's comin' along."

"Ann Debeau's bossing the job herself, I guess."

"Nope." The workman spat once more, then turned back to Colt, a twinkle in his eye. "The lady's in New York, if that's what you're asking."

"Much obliged."

"Don't mention it."

It was Ann's first show since she'd come back to New York and she was nervous.

"What do you think about this dress?" It was an

elegant blue linen column, slit on the left side. "Is it too sexy? Too plain? Maybe I should have worn chiffon."

Erica put her hands on Ann's shoulders and gently pushed her toward the door.

"You're perfect. Now get out there and work your charm on my patrons so they'll spend obscene amounts of money and make us both fabulously wealthy."

Erica had been the first person to handle Ann's work, and she'd lost count of the number of times she'd seen Ann through opening-night jitters. Once Ann stepped into the gallery, though, she was transformed. Moving among the pieces she'd created, she was alight with a true passion for her art, and her enthusiasm was contagious. Erica watched as the patrons flocked to her, eager to hear about the creative process, to ask questions, or merely to bask in Ann's glow.

Erica caught Ann's eye and gave her the thumbs-up sign.

"Bravo," she mouthed. Ann smiled at her, then leaned down to answer the question of Mrs. Gordon Palk, who had been to every one of Ann's gallery showings since her first.

"My dear, these pieces are some of the best you've ever done."

"Thank you, Mrs. Palk."

Ann welcomed the affirmation. Alone in her studio with the wet clay she had nothing except her own instincts to rely on. It pleased her to hear Mrs. Palk confirm what she'd thought.

"They're different." Mrs. Palk pointed to a free-form piece entitled "The Sea." "Such power, such passion. My dear, what was the influence?"

"Nature," she said, and it was partially true. "I experienced Hurricane Bethany at close range, and my art will never be the same."

Nor my life, she thought, but that was not the kind of thing she would tell a patron, nor anyone else for that matter. Ann laid her heart bare in her work, but in public she kept her private life closely guarded.

Mrs. Palk took her hand. "I am in awe, my dear."

"So am I."

Electrified, Ann turned slowly to face Colt Butler. He was as tall as she remembered, as fit, as deeply tanned. His hair was the same, wild and untamable, his smile still magical. Unbidden passion stole her breath.

Colt bent over her hand. "Hello, Annie." The kiss he planted in her palm sent shivers through her.

Ann knew she had an audience. Big and brash and handsome, Colt was enough to draw a crowd, but her own reaction to him didn't go unnoticed. Mrs. Palk was looking on with avid interest, as were several other longtime fans.

Ann finally found her voice. "What brings you to New York, Colt?"

"You. I want to buy the piece you call 'The Sea.'" He took her arm and led her away from the crowd. "Now, tell me again about the influence."

"You heard?"

"I did. You mentioned the hurricane, but I see something more in that piece, Annie."

Displayed in the center of the gallery, "The Sea"

sucked her in once more, and Ann felt the power, the passion, felt the water lapping against her skin, wet and cold, felt strong arms around her, felt stars exploding in her soul as they merged.

"What do you see?" she whispered.

"You and me, Annie."

SEVENTEEN

Had love of art brought Colt to New York, or love of her?

It was a question Ann didn't dare ask. She didn't want to know the answer, not yet. Her feelings were too new, her experiences too raw.

He was the last patron to leave the gallery.

"Will you two excuse me a moment?" Erica said. "I have to go to my office and tally up all the nice fat checks I received." She kissed Ann's cheek. "Thank you, thank you, darling."

Then turning to Colt, she shook his hand. "And thank you."

She left in a swirl of black taffeta and a trail of expensive perfume.

"I'm staying at the Algonquin, Annie. Will you join me?"

"Join you?"

Her face must have given away her thoughts.

"For drinks."

He couldn't have chosen a more perfect place. Seated in a plush velvet chair in a room with the original paneling rubbed to a soft patina, Ann felt the spirit of the artists who used to gather there. But as she looked across the small table at Colt, her mind wasn't on art. Far from it. Everything she'd experienced in that attic room on the bay came back to her.

She sipped her drink. "How did you know about the show?"

"Erica. I bought my first piece of Ann Debeau pottery in her gallery." He leaned back in his chair. "You look good, Annie."

"So do you."

"I saw the crew you'd sent to Windchime House."

"How does it look?"

"The outside looks great."

"I'm glad."

Like opponents in a high-stakes game of poker, they danced around, waiting to see who would stand and who would fold. Colt set his glass down, then reached across the table and traced the top of her left hand.

"No ring."

"I returned it."

"I take that as a good sign."

She smiled. "You would."

Matilda, the Algonquin cat, padded up to Colt, arched her back, and rubbed against his leg.

"You've charmed her."

Only Yesterday

His eyes darkened, and he folded her hand into his. "What about you, Annie? Have I charmed you?"

Ann didn't play games and had no patience with people who did.

"Yes," she said. "And confused me."

"As long as you think of me, that's a start."

"I think of little else, Colt. Not just you but everything that happened in Fairhope." She leaned an elbow on the table and cupped her chin. "Was it all a dream, Colt?"

"It was no dream, Annie. It was real."

"Sometimes I feel split in two," she confided. "Don't you?"

"On the contrary. I feel whole. Knowing about Anthony Chance has made me understand myself more fully."

"In the daytime when I'm working, I see flashes of my grandmother and Anthony, and at night my dreams are so vivid, I almost feel as if I've gone back again."

"I dream too."

Everything he felt shone in his eyes, and Ann was almost blinded by the force of his passion. Desire swamped her, and if she hadn't been sitting down, her knees would have buckled.

"I dream of making love with you again, Annie."

Again. Souls merged, bodies intertwined, and the sea beating against the shore.

Fools rush in, caution whispered, and she was determined not to go to Colt on the rebound, regardless of what had happened in Fairhope. To get herself under control she thought of the tranquillity of the flower garden at Windchime House. But just when her libido slowed to a trot, she thought of the roses, and she was off and running once more, her imagination taking her to places she'd never been with another man, sensual, erotic places, pleasure palaces among the stars.

"I wonder if I'm seeing those images because of what I read in Anthony's letters to my grandmother or what I experienced . . . or what I wanted to be true?"

Mesmerized, they studied each other, then he pulled back her chair.

"Come," he said.

She took his hand without hesitation. "Where are we going?"

"There's something I have to show you."

They were alone on the elevator. The air was so thick with desire that Ann felt as if she were in a sauna. His chest rose and fell as if he were running, and Ann matched her breathing to the hard rhythm of his. He laced their fingers, and made erotic circles in her palm. The pad of his thumb was slightly roughened, hot and insistent.

Waves of desire and pleasure built in her, and she bit the underside of her lip to keep from crying out.

The elevator doors hissed open, their sound as loud as a thousand snakes to her heightened senses.

"This is it."

He led her into a suite on the ninth floor, and pulled out a chair in the sitting area, but all she could see was the bed, an old-fashioned cherry four-poster, visible through the open door.

"Wait right here."

Only Yesterday

He disappeared into the bedroom while she stayed on the sofa, more conscious of her body and its raging needs than she'd ever been before.

Colt had to collect himself before he could return to the sitting room. His hunger for Annie was all-consuming, but his need for her was far more than sexual. He wanted total commitment and undying love. Nothing less would do. Nor could it be forced. Annie had to come to him of her own free will.

And so he stood in the bedroom viewing her through the door and imagining what it would be like to wake up with her beside him every morning, not sleeping across a dusty space on a chaise longue while he tossed and turned on a quilt nearby, but curled up against him in his big bed on the ranch, her hip pressed intimately against his, her hand curled in the hair on his chest, her cheek resting on his shoulder. He wanted to turn her face to the light first thing every morning and see the pink patch his shoulder would make on her skin. He wanted to rub his fingers over the spot, then kiss it softly as he watched her come awake.

He wanted to see her pad barefoot to the bathroom, her shiny hair mussed from a night of lovemaking. He wanted to watch her brush her teeth. He wanted to watch her emerge from the shower, skin glistening. He wanted to watch her dream.

For now, though, it was enough to touch her, to sit beside her and listen to the musical cadences of her voice.

"Here it is, Annie."

He set the bag on the floor, and watched her reaction. Her eyes widened, and her face turned pink.

"Anthony's bag."

"Yes. How did you know?"

"I recognized it. . . . Maybe I saw it in one of the photographs in the trunk."

"Maybe you saw it the day he left for the Pacific."

"Colt, please."

"All right. No more."

She opened the antique bag, and there on the top was a stack of yellowing letters, all addressed to Anthony Chance.

"My grandmother's letters . . . Where did you find the bag?"

"Remember those stories Pete told you about his friendship with Richard Debeau?" Spellbound, Ann nodded. "A few days ago he came into the kitchen carrying this bag. Anthony's bag. You should have seen Uncle Pete's face. He told me to tell you he's sorry he forgot to give it to you when you were there."

"But how did Anthony's bag end up with your uncle Pete?"

"The way he tells it, your grandfather brought it to him about three months after he'd married your grandmother. He said he had to get the bag out of Charlotte Ann's sight, that she cried every time she looked at it."

"Did he know whose bag it was and what was in it?"

"If he did, he never mentioned it. And of course, Pete never looked inside. He threw it into the back of his closet and forgot about it all these years, until he met you."

Knowing that Anthony's bag had been in the house where Colt Butler lived gave Ann chills. She believed that everything happened by design, not coincidence.

And yet, she still stubbornly refused to follow her heart.

She put her grandmother's letters back into Anthony's bag. It was time to go.

"How long will you be in New York, Colt?"

"Long enough."

"To conduct business? To see the shows?"

The look he gave her was eloquent, full of pent-up desire and unspoken promises.

"Long enough to convince you to go back with me."

Ann sat on her bed, one of her grandmother's letters open in her hand, the others spread around her.

Though she'd told Colt she was perfectly capable of taking a cab home, he'd insisted on coming with her. Then he'd escorted her to the door to make sure she arrived there safely. He wanted to come in and check out her apartment to be sure no muggers were lurking behind the door, but she'd pushed him back toward the cab.

He looked so forlorn as he gave her a small salute from inside the cab that she'd almost relented. Now she was glad she hadn't.

The letter she'd picked at random spoke directly to

her heart, as if Charlotte Ann Harris Debeau were standing over her granddaughter's shoulder offering advice. As Ann began to read, her grandmother's voice echoed to her down through the years . . .

"My darling Anthony, Even though I can never mail this letter, I write to you still, knowing that somewhere, somehow you'll see, and you'll understand."

The date on the letter was October 1944, two years after Anthony's death. Chill bumps raised on her arms, Ann continued to read.

"Yesterday I married Richard Debeau. He's a kind man, and he'll be good to me. We will live in the house you and I built, my darling, but the rosewood bed remains sacred, covered by a sheet. I've converted what was meant to be our bedroom into my private office. Sometimes when I'm alone I remove the sheet, lie on our rosewood bed, and imagine you're there beside me as I gaze out at the magnolia tree.

"The roses we planted thrive. I gather them by the armload and bring them into the house. The blue rose is my favorite. Remember how we celebrated after we planted it? I'll never forget, my love, just as I'll never forget you."

Ann dashed the tears out of her eyes so she could see the words.

"Richard takes me in his arms at night and makes love to me, but my heart is not in it. My heart is with you, my darling. It will be with you always and forever.

"Memories sustain me. I'm deeply grateful to you for showing me what true love is. And I'm grateful to myself, as well. If I had played by the rules, if I had sat back and analyzed instead of spurning convention and following my heart, I would never have known what real love felt like."

A knife twisted in Ann's heart. Would she ever know? Could she get past her doubts in order to find out?

"I will try and be a good wife to Richard. We will have children, God willing. Perhaps we will grow old together. But I will never cease loving you, my darling Anthony, not in this lifetime nor beyond. And if there is a way, I know that somehow, someday you will return for me. My deepest love, forever and always, Annie."

Ann folded the letter and set it on her bedside table. She would read it again before the night was over. But first she wanted to read the rest of her grandmother's letters. They were filled with details of her days waiting in Windchime House while Anthony Chance fought in the Pacific. They described the sea and the rose garden and the changing of the seasons. They mentioned her engagement ring and her daily treks to the post office and the books she read.

And always, they spoke of her undying love.

After Ann had finished the letters, she took out the contents of the bag, item by item—Anthony's uniform, his dog tags, his medals, drawings of his Annie, a diary he'd kept. And in the bottom, the antique engagement ring described in the letters, a single diamond surrounded by emeralds and rubies. Charlotte Ann Harris had placed it back in its velvet box and tucked it underneath Anthony's belongings.

Ann put the ring on a slender gold chain and fastened it around her neck. And when the morning sun began to pink the windowsill, she knew what she had to do.

Colt was at the window when the phone rang, watching the city of New York wake up. He raced to his bedside table and picked up the receiver.

"Colt?" It was Annie, her voice soft but quietly elated.

"I'm here."

"I was hoping you would be . . ." He waited, his knuckles white as he gripped the receiver. "I'm coming home next week."

"Home?"

"To Windchime House."

EIGHTEEN

He was at her door within an hour.

"Does this mean what I think it does, Annie?"

"For now, all it means is that I'm going back South, to my roots, and I'm going to live and work in Windchime House. Have you had breakfast?"

"No."

"Neither have I."

She led him into the kitchen, which confirmed all his good opinions about Annie. Fine antiques vied for space with whimsical painted furniture; windows were ceiling to floor with lots of sun pouring through; and she wasn't shy about setting her favorite things on the countertops—a cut crystal dish filled with Christmas ornaments and underneath, a scarf embroidered with bold pinks and reds and purples, edged with purple lace; a Mickey Mouse cookie jar; a silver bud vase with a single pink rose, a pewter baby's cup engraved DEBEAU.

"All this place needs is a good dog and my boots under the table," he said, promptly fulfilling one of its needs.

Balancing two coffee cups and a tray of assorted pastries, she joined him.

"I'm so glad you came, Colt."

"Are you, Annie?" He kissed her hand, which smelled like sugar sprinkles and roses. "That's good enough to eat."

He nibbled her fingertips, watching while the smile that started with her lips ended up lighting her whole face. And it was a grand morning if nothing more was accomplished except being the cause of that smile.

"Can you stay awhile?" she said.

"As long as you need me."

"I need you, Colt." Her smile turned mischievous. "There are some things a woman can't do by herself."

"Such as?"

"Lifting heavy boxes."

If it was less than he'd expected, nothing could dampen his good humor. "So that's your ploy? You're going to use me for a packhorse."

"Among other things."

"Promises, promises."

"More coffee?"

"Yes, please. It's delicious."

"Hazelnut. There's a great little gourmet coffee shop around the corner."

She leaned over to pour the coffee, and the slender chain around her neck swung forward. On the end, dangling in the sunlight, was the antique ring.

Only Yesterday

Mesmerized, Colt caught it in the palm of his hand, turning it this way and that, watching the play of sunlight on the precious stones.

"Where did you find it?" he said.

"Don't you know?"

"No."

The air was suddenly charged with energy, and the ring, suspended between them, sent sparklers that formed a small rainbow on the white tablecloth.

"The last time I saw that ring, it was another time, another place . . . You were wearing it, Annie."

Ann sat down abruptly in her chair, as if her thoughts were too heavy to carry. A whirlwind of images flashed before her—Christmas lights blinking along Royal Street, a crowded room, the auctioneer holding a board covered with black velvet, the ring from the DeMoville estate shooting fire, Anthony bidding.

Colt hurried to her side, knelt beside her, and chafed her hands.

"You're cold."

"I'm stunned. I feel as if I'm living in two different worlds. I keep expecting to be zapped back in time. I go to bed wondering if I'm going to wake up in New York or New Orleans . . . Colt, what are we going to do?"

"I have a plan."

The plan took shape as he talked. Not that he hadn't thought about their dilemma. But his thinking took a different turn from hers. He wanted the love of Ann Debeau in the twentieth century, but he also wanted the added richness of their shared history.

"Do you think it will work?" she said.

"We won't know until we try." He pulled her out of the chair and held her close for a moment. "Now, show me to those boxes. There's work to be done."

His good humor was infectious. Ann dragged boxes from the storage closet and put him in charge of packing up her studio.

A week later Ann was in Fairhope surveying the house she'd come to love. The restoration to the house was grand, but Ann's heart hurt when she looked at the devastated rose garden.

Margaret came to help unpack, wearing a bright red shirt and hammered silver necklace that had belonged to Gilly Debeau.

"I've been so excited since your call, I couldn't see straight. It just wasn't right not having a Debeau living in this house. Where do you want this clock, honey?" Margaret wasn't one to judge. If Ann wanted a tacky plastic clock among her fine antiques, she wasn't going to be the one to say otherwise.

"I'll take that. It belongs in the bedroom."

"I'll take it up. Which one, honey?" Flushed with excitement, Margaret prattled on before Ann could reply. "The front room, I hope. Lordy, it's about time somebody used that beautiful carved rosewood bed."

"Did Aunt Gilly ever sleep there?"

"Lordy, no. You'd have thought that room was a shrine the way she acted. Kept the door locked the whole time she was living here, except when she went inside to dust. She said her mother always kept it that way, and she wasn't about to desecrate Charlotte Ann's memory. It seemed a waste, if you asked me."

"It was a waste." But not in the way Margaret meant. "But I'm using the bedroom across the hall, at least for now."

Ann's color and Margaret's curiosity rose at the same time. The doorbell pealed, giving new meaning to the phrase, "saved by the bell."

Colt strode in, the sun inked in dark gold on his skin and the smell of freshly cut grass caught in his clothes.

"Miss Margaret." He tipped his butternut baseball cap in her direction, then swiveled and tipped it toward Ann. "Miss Annie."

Ann felt rejuvenated, as if she were standing in front of a stiff breeze off the bay. All of a sudden, Colt swept her up and twirled her around.

"No more work for you today, young lady."

"You have a better idea, I suppose."

"I hear three chocolate malts calling our names, and then there's a couple of fine fillies that need riding."

Margaret got her purse and the hat she'd taken to wearing in order to live up to Gilly's fine jewelry.

"I like a man who knows the emotional value of ice cream," she said.

"A woman after my own heart." Colt set Ann down, put one arm around her, the other around Margaret, and led them out the door. "And how do you feel about horses, Miss Margaret?"

"I think a ride on the back of a horse is about the next best thing to sex, and best left to the young." She tilted her head and winked at Colt. "Wish I were young."

Racing across the meadows on Starfire, Ann had to agree with Margaret. The hypnotic rhythm of the horse combined with the sweeping, majestic view, the warmth of the sun, and the nearness of Colt mesmerized her, seduced her.

Colt reined in beside a brook, then lifted her from the saddle and held on. His arms felt exactly right, and she gave herself up to the beauty and the wonder of the place, of the man.

"Annie." He buried his face in her hair, then leaned back to look at her. "I'm so glad you're home."

"So am I, Colt."

Desire built quickly between them, as it always did, but Ann pulled back and walked to the brook to toss stones into the water. Not that she didn't want him. Far from it. But until she was certain of her own mind, she didn't want to cloud the issue.

"What are you thinking, Annie?"

"That I could stay like this forever, just you and me in this tranquil spot with nothing between us except a wonderful friendship and a kind regard."

"For now, that's enough."

He knelt beside the brook and plucked a stone out of the cool water.

"Close your eyes and hold out your hand, Annie."

Only Yesterday

She felt the press of the cool, wet stone in her palm, the warmth of Colt's hand closing around hers.

"What is it?" he said. "No, don't open your eyes, not yet."

"It's a stone, a rock."

"It's more than that. Guess again. Be creative."

"Magic?"

"That's close. Feel the shape of it. No peeking. Keep your eyes closed."

She hefted the rock, judging its weight. She squeezed it, judging its mass. Then with one finger she traced the outer edge.

"It's a heart." Her voice was filled with wonder. She opened her eyes so she could see this man who could be so many things—a strong protector, a kindhearted friend, a patient suitor, and a little boy with magic in his soul.

"It's my heart, placed in your keeping, Annie."

Too full to speak, she stood on tiptoe and kissed him softly on the lips. Smiling, he tugged her back to their horses.

"Pete will be waiting for us with a big pot of chicken soup. I'll race you back to the house."

By the time he drove her back to Windchime House, a quarter moon hung so low, it looked as if it were caught on the branches of the magnolia tree, and stars spangled the sky. In the darkness the bay and the sky merged, and except for the brightness in the heavens it was hard to tell the difference between sky and sea.

The air had a crisp bite to it, a harbinger of fall.

"In New York the leaves would be turning by now," Ann said.

"Will you miss the city?"

"Not the city. Perhaps the entertainment, particularly the opera." She sat down in the swing and patted a place beside her. He pushed off with his left foot, and they swayed for a while in silence and perfect harmony.

"Hear that?" he said. Ann listened to the sound of the wind in the trees. "Nature's symphony."

"I'll have to admit it runs a close second to Pavarotti." She looked out over the bay.

"It must have been just such a night that my grandmother and Anthony swam together in the moonlight."

Colt reached for her hand. "We'll swim in the moonlight."

Ann was glad he didn't add *again*. She had fallen in love with Colt Butler. Not the way her grandmother had tumbled for Anthony Chance, but in a quiet, meandering way that felt like taking a leisurely walk through the meadow with the sun warming your skin. It was a refreshing, reassuring, life-affirming kind of love that would endure. And underneath it all was a simmering passion that could be ignited with little more provocation than a touch, a look, a smile.

True, the attraction had been there from the beginning, but when Ann let herself love this man completely, it would be Ann Debeau loving Colt Butler.

"I'm ready," she said. One of the reasons she loved him was his patience. He waited quietly for her to elaborate. "I'm ready to carry out your plan."

"You're certain about this?"

"Absolutely certain."

"Then what are we waiting for?"

He scooped her up and carried her across the threshold, and Ann added spontaneity and a sense of fun to her growing list of Colt's assets.

Not that she needed lists. Her heart clamored with the truth, and she knew it was time to follow her heart.

The ancient clock waited for them in the attic. Colt carefully glued the bottom half—the feet and tail—back to the top half—the head and the body that held the clock face.

While they waited for the glue to dry, Ann slipped behind the screen and donned her grandmother's white dress.

In Anthony's pants and shirt, Colt waited for her. A single candle burned beside the clock, and the moon laid a bright path across the dusty floor.

There was a rustle of skirt. Annie looked like a bride coming toward him.

"You can change your mind," he said.

"I won't."

She joined him in the circle of light and reached for him. Her hand was as fragile as a baby bird nesting in his.

"This might not work, Annie."

"I know that, but if I don't try to go back I'll always live with the fear that it might happen spontaneously. And I'll always wonder what would have happened if I had tried."

"Whatever happens, Annie, know that I love you." He cupped her face. "You, Annie Debeau, not some romantic notion, but the flesh-and-blood artist who walked into my life one fine summer day and demanded that I unhand her Felix the Cat clock."

He felt the tremors that ran through her, saw the light shining in her eyes, and he kissed her. Lips and hearts blended, and the moon took on an added radiance. There was magic in the air—and music, faint far-off strains of "It Had To Be You."

And in that moment Colt learned that it was possible to travel through time and space with nothing more than a touch of the lips. With Annie, other worlds opened to him, and he tasted love accumulated through the centuries, love as familiar to him as the tattered cap he put on first thing every morning and yet as startlingly fresh and unexpected as an exotic flower blooming among yellow spring daffodils.

Just this, he thought. This is enough for today.

They lingered, the sweet, tender joining giving them both strength and courage for the test that lay ahead. And at last when they broke apart, her face was as radiant as the moon.

Colt took her hand, and they knelt beside the clock.

"Hold tight, Annie. I won't let you go."

Her smile was rich with wisdom. "I know."

Together they reached toward the clock. Fingers

contacted plastic, dust swirled like fog, and the moon faded. The air was electric with anticipation. Colt's heart raced, and he squeezed Annie's hand.

She squeezed back.

Outside an owl called, his haunting two-note melody echoing through the attic, and in the distance a dog howled. There was a crash, then the shattering of glass.

Colt held his breath, expecting at any minute to feel himself set down in unfamiliar territory. But the attic walls stood firmly around him; the creaking floor stayed beneath his feet. And under his hand was the old clock. He rubbed the black plastic. He thought of Anthony Chance and Charlotte Ann Harris. He pictured the iron balcony in New Orleans and the sun-dappled bed where they'd first made love.

But nothing happened. No amount of thinking or wishing or hoping would transport him to another place, another time.

"Colt? I don't feel anything. Do you?"

"Only you, Annie." He squeezed her hand. "I guess we've learned all they had to teach us."

Suddenly she began to laugh, and then she pulled him up and began to waltz around the room, humming, "It Had To Be You," off-key.

Her gauzy dress billowed around her legs, and his white shirt glowed in the flickering candle. Except for their full-bodied laughter, they might have been ghosts swaying and swirling and dipping.

Annie started up the song once more, then ended in a wheeze of laughter.

"You sing," she said.

And he didn't ask how she knew he could; he merely took over in a mellow baritone that filled up the attic with song.

Their waltz took them past the shelves where they'd first found the clock, and there, toppled to the floor, was an old glass canning jar, and they began to laugh again.

"I thought it was the attic window," Annie said when they stopped for breath. "I kept expecting to end up in the New Orleans Public Library or on Bourbon Street or on the streetcar."

"I was thinking of the apartment in the Quarter, the wrought-iron railing, the sun falling across the bed."

The air became electric once more, not with the mysteries of time travel but with the mysteries of love. And suddenly she was in his arms, his lips on hers, her hips fitted closely to his.

There was hunger in the kiss, hot and insistent, and desire so raw, it took their breath away.

"Do you know how much I wanted you when we were stuck here for three days?" he said when he could speak. "I thought I would go crazy lying beside you and not being able to have you."

"I wanted you, too, but I was honor bound to another man."

He had never loved her more than in that moment, for he knew that a woman bound by honor was a treasure beyond compare.

He pulled her into his arms and they kissed until

Only Yesterday

they were both breathless. Moonbeams caught in her dark hair and turned her skin to silver, and she stepped into the bright path, eyes gleaming. One by one she unfastened the tiny pearl buttons on the front of her bodice. Colt's heart slammed into his ribs.

The fabric whispered over her skin, sliding downward to reveal shoulders as pure as alabaster and breasts as rich and inviting as cream.

"For you," she said, cupping them upward.

His mouth closed over one creamy globe, and he took her sacred offering with reverence and with awe. Until that moment he'd never known that a woman could literally crawl inside a man's skin, that the blood of lovers could merge and flow together in a singing river, that breaths could blend and form angel wings that stirred the air around them.

He moved from one breast to the other in heady exploration, and she arched her back, giving him easy access. The ring lay between her breasts, chain gleaming, jewels shooting fiery sparks.

He kissed the ring, then tenderly placed it back in her cleavage and slid her dress over her hips. Her panties were a wisp of lace that invited his attention. He mouthed the silk, wet it with his tongue, then pressed inward and upward. Silk, heat, friction, dampness.

Moaning, hips writhing, she tangled her hands in his hair and held him close.

"I love you," she said.

"Who do you love?"

"You."

"Say my name."

"Colt Butler. I love you, Colt Butler."

And then there was no more conversation, for they were driven by a passion so strong, it had survived two lifetimes.

Colt pulled the antique quilt from the trunk and spread it on the floor. Her dress pooled at her feet, and his clothes joined the heap. Then, taking her hand, he led her to the quilt and lay down beside her. Facing, they traced each other with hands and lips, tasting, touching, admiring, exclaiming.

She caressed him with her hands, seared him with her lips, and wave after wave of passion crashed through him. He wanted every inch of his skin touching hers. He wanted to be melded to her so that it was impossible to tell where he left off and she began.

Lifting her hips, he dipped his tongue inside, tasting, teasing, sucking. The tremors started in her belly, spread downward through her legs, and she cried out her pleasure as the hard shudders racked her.

"Please, please," she said, reaching for him. "Now."

Poised over her, he delved briefly inside with the tip of his shaft. She arched, seeking, wanting, crying out his name. He slid into her, deep inside her hot, wet folds. Joy exploded within him, and he knew that at last he had come home.

With a rhythm as old as time, Colt Butler claimed his Annie.

And in the heavens two stars merged, coming together to form a bright orb as big as a baseball.

NINETEEN

Lying on the quilt, the ring nestled between her breasts, Colt's arm around her shoulder, her cheek on his chest, Annie felt rich and full and truly loved. She sighed with contentment.

"I don't know why I waited so long," she said.

Colt chuckled. "You always save the best for last, Annie."

She kissed the indentation right over his heart, lingering long enough to inhale his clean male scent. The fine sprinkling of dark hairs tickled her nose, and she sat up, smiling.

Through the window, the moon beckoned.

"You know what I'd like to do?" she said.

"Tell me."

"Down at the end of the walkway and around the curve there's a hidden cove . . ."

"What are we waiting for?"

Laughing like naughty children, they dressed, then

ran hand in hand to the beach. When they reached the hidden cove they cast aside their clothes and raced into the water.

"Brrr. It's cold." Ann wrapped her arms around herself, shivering. "Whose idea was this?"

"Minx. Come here. I'll warm you up."

Legs and arms tangled, bodies touched, floated apart, made contact once more.

"And just how do you propose to do that, I wonder?"

"Do you want me to tell you or show you?"

"You could put it in a letter." Laughing, she wrapped herself tightly around him. "Or you could . . ."

Her eyes widened, and she had neither time nor desire to finish the sentence. They rode the waves, rode each other, fast and furious, their hunger driving them to new heights of passion. They cried out their completion at the same time.

Back on the beach they dressed hastily and he held her tightly until the urgent rhythm of their hearts slowed. The moon bathed them in a luminescence, and Ann tipped her face upward. Colt kissed her, parting her lips softly, sucking them tenderly.

"I want to marry you, Annie."

"The answer is yes." She traced the dear lines of his face. "Yes, yes, yes."

They sealed the promise with a kiss that heated them both up enough so they didn't notice the chill of the night breeze off the bay. Then slowly Annie unfastened the chain from around her neck and slid the antique ring off.

Colt studied her face for a long time, and she nodded. There was no need for words between them; the ring said it all.

With the ring Anthony Chance had given to his Annie Harris, Colt pledged his love to his Annie Debeau. He slid it on her finger, then kissed her knuckles.

"I love you, Annie. Forever and always."

The new star sent a shaft of such brilliance over them that they felt as if they'd been touched by fire.

"Look," Annie said, pointing upward.

"I consider that a good sign."

Her white dress whispered secrets as they walked back to Windchime House, hand in hand.

Pete was the first person to hear the news.

The day after he'd proposed, Colt picked up Annie and drove her to the ranch. Pete was in the barn rubbing down the newest addition to their string of polo ponies, a stallion as black as night.

"Just delivered him yesterday," he said when he saw Ann. "Bought him from a fella in Louisiana. Isn't he a beauty?"

"Hello, Pete." She kissed his cheek, and he turned the color of a red turnip.

To cover his embarrassed pride, Pete focused on Colt. "Shame on you for not telling me you were bringing Ann out here. I'd have fried a chicken.

There's not a thing to eat in the house except peanut butter and jelly."

"I think that'll make a fine celebration, don't you, Annie?" Colt winked at her.

Once Pete got on a roll, he was like a locomotive racing downhill with his brakes gone.

"I might even have baked a cake. There's a new recipe in *Southern Living* I've been wanting to try . . . Did you say celebration?"

The hopeful look he gave Colt melted Annie's heart. She held out her left hand, and Pete teared up.

"I've been waiting for this day ever since he was old enough to shave. I couldn't be happier that it's you." He bent and kissed her hand with the gallantry of a true Southern gentleman. "Welcome to the family, my dear."

She wrapped him in a bear hug. "I'm honored, Uncle Pete."

Pete beamed as if he'd invented engagements. "When's the wedding?"

"June," they both said, then looked at each other and laughed.

"I guess you've got it all planned."

"Not yet," she said.

"I hope you don't have all these newfangled ideas about getting married in malls and on beaches and in pastures."

"Pete, are you going to be a pain in the rear about the wedding?" Colt asked.

"Yep. I'm old and I've earned the privilege."

"If Annie wants to marry on top of the haystack, that's fine with me."

"I never heard of such foolishness."

"Now, Uncle Pete, it's her wedding. I'll marry her any where and any way she wants to."

"Didn't I teach you anything? There's such a thing as sacred vows."

"Gentlemen, please!" Annie held up her hands in mock consternation. "I'm getting married in the church, and that's that."

"See, I told you." Pete gave Colt a smug look, then linked his hand through Ann's arm and led her toward the house. "You can fix up the east wing any way you want it. I'll call the painters tomorrow. I figure you might like yellow."

"When you don't want him to, he moves with the speed of light." Colt winked at Annie. "Slow down, Uncle Pete. June's a long way off."

"Too far, if you ask me."

"Mother's in Paris, and I still have lots of work to do on Windchime House . . ."

"Windchime House?" Pete gave Colt an aggrieved look. "You won't be living here?"

"There are a lot of details to be worked out, Uncle Pete. Annie and I both love Windchime House. She plans to keep it, and I have to hire a manager for the ranch . . ."

"Since when? You and I've been running this place for as long as Buck was a puppy. I don't reckon I need any help."

"I'm starving," Annie said. "Why don't I make the

sandwiches and you two scout up something cool to drink."

Later that evening after Colt drove her home he said, "I guess I should have prepared him."

"That's all right. He's a little bit scared, that's all. You're all he's got, Colt."

"He'll come around when he figures out that grandchildren will be a part of the bargain."

Ann was floating on air. The only time she and Rob had discussed children, he'd said they'd have to wait and see, that their careers came first.

She wanted children, and lots of them. She wanted to fill Windchime House and Colt's ranch with the sound of children's laughter.

Colt looked so pleased with himself that she couldn't resist teasing him.

"You want children?"

"You don't?"

The look on his face reminded her of a little boy who'd been told he couldn't have a dog for Christmas.

"I don't know."

She had to stifle laughter at the way he was valiantly trying to cover his disappointment. She decided to let him off the hook.

"I've never had any," she added, "so I'm not sure I know how. . . . Do you think we could practice?"

"You're a regular little stand-up comic." He scooped her up and bounded up the stairs, two at a time. "What I ought to do is give you a dose of your own medicine."

He strode through her bedroom door and kicked the door shut.

"My, that sounds ominous. Should I be afraid?"

"Only if you're scared of being loved to death."

"Is that a promise?"

"That's a promise."

"What a way to go."

Her bed, a regular-size wrought-iron she'd had shipped from New York, was far too small for the likes of Colt Butler. But that didn't stop him from making good on his promise.

The little bed rocked and groaned and threatened to collapse, and later as she lay curved against him she wondered how it was possible for one woman to have so very much . . . wonderful friends, a great career, a grand old house, and a man who made her feel like a princess.

Without warning, the plane plunging into the Pacific whispered across her mind and she shivered.

"Cold?" Colt held her tighter and pulled the sheet over her bare shoulders.

"I was just thinking about Charlotte Ann and Anthony. Are we tempting the Fates with all this happiness?"

"Shh." He soothed her by stroking her hair. "Don't think like that. June is not so far away, and before you know it, we'll be old and gray and sitting on the front porch swing wondering where all the years went."

"And what might we be doing on that front porch swing?"

"Did you have anything in mind?"

She reached for his hand and intertwined their fingers. "This might be nice."

"It might."

"And this . . ." She trailed kisses down the side of his face.

"I like that too. Any other ideas?"

She stroked his chest, then downward, where she made a remarkable discovery.

"How about this?" She threw back the covers and lowered herself onto his rigid shaft.

"Are you sure we can do this in the front porch swing?"

"Only if it's a dark and moonless night."

She began to rock and sway above him, and there was no more talk for a very long time.

Ann was caught in a whirlwind of activities, settling in, getting back into her work, planning her wedding. September gave way to October, and the air was crisp with excitement. Point Clear's charity polo match to benefit children's cancer research was in the offing, and celebrities from around the world descended on south Alabama to participate.

"I've never seen a polo match," Ann told Colt.

"I'm glad you'll see me ride in your first."

The day of the match turned out to be glorious and golden, with sunshine bathing the polo fields and causing the spectators to shed their sweaters. Ann sat with Uncle Pete in the bleachers, sharing a bag of popcorn.

"Popped it this morning over the fireplace," he said. "I always come prepared. These things can make you chew your fingernails if you don't have something else to occupy your mouth."

"It's delicious."

Her ring sparkled as she dug into the buttery popcorn, and she smiled. Margaret, who was coming two days a week to help her organize her house and her mail and had become an unofficial girl Friday, told her she was doing a lot of that lately.

"I have more to smile about than I ever dreamed possible," Ann had told her.

Was it yesterday? Or last week? Time seemed to fly, and as far as Ann was concerned, it couldn't fly fast enough.

"Here they come," Uncle Pete said.

Horses' hooves thundered on the green turf, and Ann scanned the players for Colt. It didn't take her long to find him, even without Uncle Pete's help. Tall and proud, he rode head and shoulders above the rest.

"There he is." Uncle Pete pointed, then stood up and waved his cap. "Handsomest stallion out there."

"I couldn't agree more."

"I'm talking about the horse." Uncle Pete chuckled.

"The horse is handsome too."

Now that Pete was used to the idea of Colt and Annie dividing their time between Windchime House and the ranch, he and Annie had developed an easy rapport, if not an outright mutual admiration society.

"I wished he was up on Warrior. You should have seen the two of them play. I've never known man and horse to be so in tune with each other." Pete reached for the popcorn. "Of course, Colt can make any horse look good. He's got the biggest handicap of any player on that field."

"That's terrible," Ann said.

Pete grinned. "No. That's good. The best players have the highest handicaps."

"I guess I have a lot to learn about polo."

"Don't worry, young 'un. Married to my boy, you'll sure learn fast."

The first period began, called a chukker, Pete told her, and Ann was on the edge of her seat the entire time, knuckles white around the bag of popcorn.

"It's dangerous," she said when the first chukker ended and the players rode off the field to change to fresh mounts.

"Yep."

"It's exciting, of course, but I'm not so sure I like this sport."

"Colt's mama never could get used to it, God rest her soul."

"What happened to his parents? Colt never said."

When Pete told her, Ann felt the blood drain from her face. Fear pulsed through her.

Pete patted her hand. "Now, now. There's no need for you to worry. Colt knows what he's doing." As the

Only Yesterday

horses thundered onto the field once more, Pete added, "I sure hope that horse does."

Ann was in a full frenzy now, her imagination running wild.

"What do you mean? What's wrong with that horse?"

"Nothing. This is the stallion's first game, that's all." He patted her hand. "You don't have a thing to worry about. I trained that horse myself, and Colt is better than Tommy Hitchcock, Jr."

"Who's he?"

"The greatest polo player of all time."

Ann found out she couldn't hold her breath the whole game, but in spite of the melee on the field, she never took her eyes off Colt.

"Want some corn?" Uncle Pete said, but she never heard him.

When the final chukker ended, she felt as limp as a rag doll. Victorious, Colt tore off his helmet, strode toward the bleachers, and swung her into his arms.

"How did you like your first game?"

"Now that it's over, great."

"Poor baby, we'll have to think of something to soothe your ruffled feathers."

They had a victory dinner of Pete's chicken and dumplings.

"I was more worried about Annie than I was about you," Pete told Colt. "Take her out and show her the horses. Once she gets to know them maybe she'll feel better about the game."

"I couldn't have come up with a better idea myself."

The barn was warm and cozy and smelled of leather and fresh hay and horseflesh. Colt bolted the barn door, pulled her down into a fragrant haystack, and began to unbutton her blouse.

"What about the horses?" she said, teasing him.

"Let them find their own girl."

His mouth closed over her breast, and Annie forgot everything except the wonder of love.

By the time she'd seen her third game, Ann began to relax and enjoy polo. And she was Colt's biggest fan. Every time he scored she tore her hat off and waved it, cheering.

Pete, a staunch believer in not tempting fate, insisted Annie wear the same hat to every game, saying there was no use jeopardizing a winning streak.

"Where's your lucky hat?" he asked as they settled in their places on the bleachers.

It was a gray misty day with rain clouds scudding across the sky and occasionally spitting a few drops onto the polo field.

"It's here." Ann patted the canvas bag that also contained sunglasses, in case of a change of weather, and a large supply of chocolate bars. Ann craved chocolate when she got excited, and she'd been excited a lot lately.

"If I keep going to these polo games, I'm going to

get fat as a pig," she'd told Colt last night. They were curled side by side on her sofa in front of a cozy fire.

"And I'm going to love every extra inch."

"Even a spare tire?"

"Show me."

She pulled off her sweater to display a midriff he declared was as flat as a wheat field in Kansas. And then he'd spent a considerable amount of time showing her exactly how he planned to appreciate her extra fat.

Thinking of their evening together put Ann in such a mellow, dreamy mood that Pete had to get her attention when the players came onto the field. Ann grabbed her hat out of the bag, waved it at Colt, then blew him a big kiss.

"I guess you love him."

"I guess I do."

"Well, then, put your lucky hat on. We can't let him down."

Pete couldn't seem to stop grinning these days, especially when Ann was around. If he'd been picking out a wife for Colt himself, he couldn't have made a better choice.

A light rain started falling during the third chukker, and tricky maneuvers of horse and rider became even more challenging on the wet turf. But that didn't stop the players. Colt charged down the field time and again, leaning low over his horse, mallet swinging as he scored for his team.

During the fifth chukker the rain picked up speed. Mud spewed behind the polo ponies as they thundered over the field and spattered their leg boots. The brim of Ann's hat began to droop, and she had to keep lifting it out of her way.

"Next time I'll bring a rain hat," she said.

"Can't. It wouldn't be your lucky hat."

She was laughing when Colt galloped down the field, in possession of the ball, racing for another goal. An opposing player charged in, angling in front of Colt in a desperate effort to block the goal.

"Watch him, watch him," Pete said, his voice low and urgent.

There was the sound of impact, horseflesh meeting horseflesh. Ann jerked out of her seat, her mouth wide open in a scream that got trapped in the back of her throat.

Colt tilted in his saddle, almost lost his seating. But he was still on the horse, hanging on by sheer will. And he still had the ball.

Later no one would be able to describe what had happened next, least of all Ann. Everything blurred, like a movie reel going too fast. Images exploded through her mind like cannon shot—mud spraying, horses colliding, somebody screaming, wood splintering, somebody on the ground.

"Colt," she screamed. It was Colt on the ground, lying as still as death.

There was a flash of lightning, flames, a wide expanse of cold gray water, and a plane spiraling downward, carrying Anthony with it.

"Nooo!"

Rivulets streamed down her face, and she didn't know if it was rain or tears. Nor did she care. The only thing that mattered was that history was repeating itself.

The man she loved more than life itself lay in the rain, silent and unmoving, and Ann's whole world crashed around her feet.

"Get up," Pete was saying. "Get up."

Ann's brim flopped into her face, and she clawed her hat off her head and threw it into the mud. On the field horses milled, riders tried to quiet them, and Colt didn't move.

Annie screamed his name. "Oh God, he can't die."

She had to get to him. He had to be all right.

The crowd huddled closer together, as if the bodies of strangers could give them comfort in a tragedy. Ann began to push her way through the crowd.

"Annie, wait." Pete clutched her sleeve. "You can't go down there. It's dangerous."

"I don't care." She jerked free. "I have to go to him. Don't you understand?"

She pushed forward once more, but Pete caught her arm in a firm grip and held her fast.

"He's getting help, Annie."

White coats flapped in the rain as paramedics raced toward a waiting ambulance bearing the weight of a laden gurney. Colt was so still, so silent. Ann pressed her face into her hands and wept.

"Come on, sweetheart." He led her off the bleachers, parting the spectators. "Out of my way. That's my boy."

The ambulance doors were closing when Pete and Annie emerged from the crowd.

"Wait," he yelled. "We're riding with him."

"Come on, then. Hurry!"

The door swung open, and Pete and Ann climbed into the back of the ambulance. Colt lay motionless, paramedics on either side, one checking his blood pressure, the other his pupils.

Pete squeezed her hand. "Be strong, Annie."

She'd lost him once and by some miracle, he'd come back to her. Annie didn't think she could endure the pain if she lost him a second time.

Seeing her face, one of the paramedics motioned, then made room for her. She caught Colt's hand, then leaned down.

"I'm here, darling. And I'm not going to let you go. Do you hear me, Colt Butler? Don't you dare leave me."

Her command was as fierce as her face, but there was no response from the gurney, not even the flicker of an eyelash. A scream welled up from her throat, but Ann pushed it firmly back in place.

There would be no more screams, she vowed. Not one.

Colt's face was muddy, his hair damp. She pulled out her shirttail and tenderly wiped his face, then, leaning close, she pressed her lips over his.

TWENTY

Colt stirred, then his eyes popped open. Ann wept with joy.

"I knew you'd come back," she whispered, smothering his face with kisses. "I knew it."

"Where've I been?" he said.

The ambulance pulled up to the emergency room, and there wasn't time for more conversation. Ann and Pete sat anxiously in the waiting room while a team of doctors pored over Colt.

Time crept. Ann thumbed through out-of-date magazines and counted the number of chairs and wondered why hospitals always chose colors that looked like the interiors of caskets.

Her heart jumped into her throat when Dr. Samuel Whitfield approached them.

"How is he? Is it serious? Is he going to be all right?"

She was so anxious, the questions spilled out. Pete

wasn't much better. He had a nervous tic under his eye and he'd passed his hands over his face so much, his eyebrows had puffed up like hydrangea bushes in full bloom.

"What's the bottom line, Doc?" His voice was gruff to cover his emotion. "In plain language, please."

"Concussion. Cracked ribs. His ribs are going to be sore, and he's a little addled right now. Don't be alarmed if the confusion lasts awhile, but your boy is going to be as good as new."

"I could kiss you," Ann said, and she did.

"Best payment I've had all day."

"When can we see him?" Pete said.

"As soon as he gets settled into his room. We're going to keep him overnight for observation."

Colt was in jail and furthermore somebody had taken his clothes and left him in a ridiculous gown that barely covered his butt. And he was raging mad.

The only good thing was that they'd let his uncle Pete visit him, and he'd brought a beautiful woman who was vaguely familiar. Annie, he'd heard Pete call her.

"You tell that warden I want my clothes," he told Uncle Pete.

"I'll go tell him right now." Pete winked at Annie, then strolled from the room.

"Are you comfortable?" Annie said.

She smoothed the sheet over his chest and fiddled

with his pillow. He had no idea what she was doing in the jail, but she smelled so good and looked so great that almost made his incarceration worthwhile.

"Haven't we met somewhere before?" he said.

"We've met."

"I thought so."

She touched him lightly on the cheek, and he reacted to her in an embarrassingly personal way. If he hadn't been in that stupid gown, he might have done something about it.

"What are you doing here?" he said.

"Taking care of you."

"I can see that. I mean what are you in for?"

"Colt, don't you know me?"

"You're Annie."

"That's right. And what else?"

"You smell good." He grinned at her.

Uncle Pete came back in empty-handed, Colt noticed. He'd have to go have a talk with the warden himself. He threw back his covers, and swung his legs over the side of the bed, but a dizzy spell sent him reeling backward.

"Whoa there." Uncle Pete pulled the covers back over him. "You won't be going anywhere for a while."

He didn't argue. His ribs felt like somebody had taken a sledgehammer to them, and his head didn't feel all that good either.

"Just rest." Annie put a cool hand on his brow, and it felt so good, he covered her hand to hold it there.

He was just drifting into sleep, when he remembered what had been bothering him for the last few minutes. He sat up and glared at Uncle Pete.

"I'm not going to the dentist, and that's final."

Pete went home to take care of the horses, but Ann insisted on staying with Colt. She keep her vigil in a chair beside his bed.

"Can we bring you a cot for tonight?" the nurse said.

"No, thank you. I'll be fine right here." Ann wasn't about to leave his side. She wanted to be close enough to touch him.

As the moon tracked across the sky she watched the rise and fall of his breathing and occasionally felt the steady thrum of his pulse, anxious for any signs of change.

What if the doctors were wrong? What if he'd suffered some kind of irreversible brain damage?

Exhausted, she closed her eyes, but visions of the accident on the polo field came to her, and she jerked herself awake. She smoothed his hair back from his forehead, then kissed him softly.

"Don't stay away too long, my love. I'm bereft without you."

The hospital's night sounds drifted through the door—soft swish of rubber-soled shoes on polished linoleum, the rattle of a cart, discreet tapping on doors, the distant ring of the telephone. Ann nodded off, her head falling to her chest, then jerked herself awake.

Finally, mindful of Colt's bandaged chest, she laid her head on the side of his bed and slept.

His hand in her hair woke her.

"Annie? What did the doctor say about me? I can't seem to remember."

"Colt! You know who I am."

He cupped her cheek with one hand. "Aren't you the same beautiful woman who promised to marry me?"

"I was scared to death. I thought I'd lost you."

"Come here." He pressed her head onto his chest and stroked her hair. "Better?"

"Yes. Much better."

There was a long silence as both of them thought how close they'd come to losing their dream.

"Annie . . . unless you're sentimentally attached to June, what would you say about a winter wedding?"

"I would say you'd better hurry and get completely well then, because I don't fancy taking a beat-up man to my wedding bed."

"If it weren't for an audience outside the door, I'd show you what a beat-up man can do."

She laughed. "Promises, promises."

TWENTY-ONE

They were married on Christmas Eve. A cold front hit Fairhope, and wedding guests bundled into winter coats and complained about the forty-degree weather as they gathered at the small white church for the evening ceremony. The night was clear, the sky full of stars. One star in particular stood out, and some folks remarked that it must be the star that led the wise men to the Christ child.

But Annie and Colt knew better. For one thing, the star was in the wrong side of the sky. For another, two unusually bright stars hung in the winter-black sky—but only one of them was as big as a baseball.

The organ pealed, and Annie walked down the aisle in the dress Charlotte Ann Harris had bought for her marriage to Anthony Chance. In front of the altar was the man who had waited two lifetimes to be with her.

Joy sang through her as she took his hand.

"Dearly beloved, we are gathered here to unite this

man and this woman in holy wedlock," the minister said, beginning the ceremony.

And when Colt slid a band encrusted with diamonds, rubies, and emeralds on her finger, and she heard the miraculous words, "I now pronounce you man and wife," Ann knew that at last she'd truly come home.

Pete hosted a reception at the ranch. Ann's mother, Lisa, who had flown in from Paris with her husband Charlie Chastain, had argued for a country club affair, but Pete stood his ground. He wasn't about to give over to somebody who didn't have the good grace to show up until everything was done except the shouting, and he told her so.

Colt and Annie watched as Lisa and Pete circled each other like gladiators in a Roman arena.

"Do you think they'll ever make peace?" she said.

"You can count on it." He kissed his bride's hand. "When the first grandchild comes, they'll be in cahoots up to their eyebrows, both of them trying to tell us what to do."

"Speaking of babies . . ." Eyes gleaming with mischief, she stood on tiptoe and whispered something in his ear.

"What? Practice again? With a party going on?"

"Of course, if you'd rather dance—"

Annie never got to finish her sentence. Colt scooped her up and strode toward the door.

"If you're going to throw that bouquet, now's the time, Annie."

She tossed it straight toward Margaret, who was decked out in Gilly's pearls and a velvet hat Gilly had brought from Paris, and who had spent the first hour of the reception eyeing Pete and the last hour trying to work up her courage to flirt with him.

Rice pelted over them as they waved good-bye to friends and relatives. Though the word was out that they would honeymoon off the coast of Maine, Colt and Annie drove straight to Windchime House.

It was hauntingly beautiful in the winter darkness. A full moon illuminated the stately white columns and transformed the fanlight over the front door to sparkling crystal. Moss swayed, ghostlike from the live oak trees, and a single star perched on top of the magnolia tree as if it had been put there by the hand of an angel.

They stood hand in hand and viewed the house that had been built for love.

"Welcome home, my darling," Annie whispered.

Colt cradled her in his arms and carried her across the threshold. A shining path lay on the staircase, and as they ascended Annie's wedding gown looked like moonbeams.

Annie's bedroom was at the top of the landing on the left, her wrought-iron bed visible through the open door. Colt strode to the opposite side of the hallway and pushed open the door.

Through the wide French windows was the magnolia tree and a sweeping view of the bay. A comfortable tuxedo sofa and plush velvet chairs made an inviting sitting area, and opposite stood Charlotte Ann Harris's antique desk. But the centerpiece of the room was the bed, draped in white.

The hush in the room was almost sacred. Colt set Annie tenderly on the floor, and they stood hand in hand looking at the veiled bed.

"That bed has been waiting a long time," Annie said.

Colt squeezed her hand. "So have we."

They glanced at each other, and words were not necessary. Colt took one end of the sheeting and Annie took the other, and slowly they unveiled the bed.

Annie ran her hand over the intricately carved roses, the intertwined vines, the exquisite leaves.

"It's so beautiful," she said.

"So are you, Mrs. Butler."

Colt lit candles around the room, then lifted her onto the bed. Her white gown billowed around her like foam on the sea. He knelt above her and bracketed her shoulders with his hands.

"I have loved you since the first time I ever laid eyes on you, and I will love you forever."

"And I love you," she whispered, reaching for him. "Forever and always."

The buttons on her antique wedding gown were tiny and hard to unfasten, but Colt didn't hurry. He had a lifetime and beyond to love this woman.

He peeled her gown away by inches, christening each bit of exposed flesh with lips and tongue. His touch electrified her, and she arched upward. She wove her fingers through his hair as his mouth closed around one erect nipple, and she rocked and murmured to some ancient inner rhythm as he suckled.

Her body ripened and quickened as he moved downward. She strained toward his questing tongue, shattering like cut crystal. Bits and pieces exploded through her. Fragmented, she ripped open his shirt, shoved aside his pants, seeking the magic that would make her whole.

The moon turned her body to silver, and he was the flame tempering it white-hot. With the ancient bedposts standing sentinel and their bodies pressed into the downy mattress, the lovers branded each other, knowing that no matter what the future brought, they belonged together for all eternity.

Much later, wrapped in her husband's arms, Annie said, "Do you think Charlotte Ann and Anthony know?"

Colt turned his face to the window, and seeing the brightness at the top of the magnolia tree, he smiled.

"They know," he said.

TWENTY-TWO

Spring burst upon Fairhope with an ostentatious display of color that shamed the rest of the country. Forsythia dripped yellow starflowers onto the greening grass; azaleas mushroomed in shades ranging from frothy pink to deep purple; hawthorn rouged itself with tiny red blooms; the redbuds vied for attention with flower-laden branches. And everywhere dogwood flowered snowlike.

Margaret stood at the window of Annie's studio in Windchime House, admiring spring's show.

"It's enough to make a body feel young again." She turned from the window, her cheeks glowing with natural color as if she'd made her own prediction come true.

"It's a time of birth and renewal," Annie agreed. Sitting at her wheel, her hands covered with clay, she gave a secret smile.

"Ann, there's something I've been wanting to ask

you for two weeks, and I've just now got up the courage."

The bond they'd forged when Ann came to Fairhope to close up Gilly's estate had become stronger over the months, almost as strong as the one between Gilly and Margaret.

"You can ask me anything or tell me anything, Margaret. You know that."

"You don't know how much that means to me, how much you mean to me. Your aunt Gilly would be so proud of you." Margaret pulled a handkerchief out of her purse and blew her nose.

"I just wish she had lived to see your wedding, and you and Colt living in this house, and all."

"Maybe she did," Annie said softly.

Margaret moved closer to the wheel so she could watch the work in progress. When she'd first started paying neighborly visits to Windchime House, Annie would stop in the middle of whatever she was doing to entertain. But Margaret had protested vigorously, saying the best entertainment she knew of was watching Annie shape clay into works of art.

"What's that going to be?" Margaret said.

"A surprise for Colt . . . and you'll be the first to see."

Margaret looked as if she'd been named Citizen of the Year.

"Where is he, by the way?"

"Gone to Kentucky to bring back a polo pony."

"Don't you worry, after what happened?"

"Never. My life is too full of wonderful things for

worry. Besides, I would never try to deprive Colt of something that makes him so happy."

Annie turned the wheel, shaping the clay, and Margaret watched for a while, then cleared her throat. Annie smiled. That was a signal that Margaret was getting ready to say what was really on her mind.

"If I was to go into Mobile to a symphony concert, what do you think I ought to wear?"

"Anything goes nowadays. You can dress for comfort or style. Either way is acceptable."

"If I dress for style, what do you think would be the most stylish on me. Truthfully, now. I don't want to look like some old biddy trying to look half her age."

"How about that lovely black sheath you have, with pearls?"

"Don't you think black makes me look a little old?"

It wasn't like Margaret to fidget and fuss so over something as simple as going to the symphony. What was going on?

"Wear that lovely red linen suit, then. Everybody looks younger in red."

"Don't you think a suit is a little too severe?" Margaret drew her compact out of her purse, inspected her hair, and tucked a stray strand into her bun. "Maybe you could help me buy a nice cocktail dress. In blue."

"Of course I will. Margaret, is there something you're not telling me?"

"Somebody is taking me to the concert. Somebody I want to impress."

"Would this be somebody I know?" While she waited for Margaret to get up the nerve to answer,

Annie shut down the power and took her piece off the wheel.

"Pete," Margaret said.

Being careful of her muddy hands, Annie hugged her. "That's the best news I've had in a long time."

"Speaking of news . . ." Margaret inspected Annie's newest piece of greenware. "Is that a baby's cup?"

"Yes."

They hugged once more, then Margaret let out a yelp. "Would you look a-yonder! I thought he was in Kentucky."

Annie raced to the window, and pulling into the yard was Colt Butler, driving a yellow flatbed truck loaded with roses.

"That man," Annie said. "He's wonderfully, beautifully mad."

Margaret picked up her purse and started to the door.

"You don't have to go, do you?"

"I may not know much, but I know when two's company and three's a crowd."

Colt parked the truck under the magnolia tree, next to the rose beds that had been destroyed in Hurricane Bethany. Margaret came down the front steps as he barreled out of the truck and he waved.

"How's it going, Margaret?"

"Never better."

She drove off, and he went inside whistling. Annie

was at the top of the stairs, and he took them two at a time and scooped her up.

"What would you say, Mrs. Butler, if I told you that I have a rainbow under the magnolia tree?"

"*Under* the tree?"

Her smile was the most radiant thing he'd ever seen, and he felt as if he were ten feet tall.

"That's right, Mrs. B. Under the tree. It's a wonder to behold. Would you like to see for yourself?"

"Absolutely."

He started down the stairs then stopped on the fifth stair. "Wait, am I forgetting something?"

She smelled like roses, and he couldn't carry out the game any longer. He crushed his mouth over hers, and they stayed on the fifth stair for a very long time.

"There now," he said. "That's better."

She wove her hands in his hair. "Welcome home, darling."

He started down the stairs once more, but stopped on the fourth, third, second, and first stairs to repeat the welcoming process.

"At this rate, I'll never see that rainbow."

"Are you complaining?"

"No, bragging. Do you intend to carry me all the way?"

"All the way." Three days away from her felt like forever, and he had a lot of catching up to do.

He hurried through the doorway, then down the porch steps and around the corner of the flatbed truck. She gasped with pure pleasure.

"There's the rainbow, Annie. What do you think?"

The truck was loaded with pots, and in those pots were roses of every color and kind.

"I think you're the most wonderful man alive. Oh, Colt, you knew how much I missed the roses."

"You like them, then?" The question was rhetorical. Her face glowed as if she'd been set loose in heaven.

"I adore them!"

He set her down, and she raced around the truck, counting pots and exclaiming over the varieties.

"Colt . . . fifty-nine rosebushes."

"You missed one."

He leaned over her and plucked a potted rose from behind a white English hybrid tea. Tight buds covered the bush, but at the top a single rose bloomed, as blue as Colt Butler's eyes.

A vision flashed before them—a windswept hill, a sea bright with sun diamonds, and two people waltzing in front of a newly built house. Paints lay on the grass beside them, and the woman's dress fluttered and soared like the wings of a dozen white doves.

In an instant the image vanished, and Colt plucked the single blue rose and tucked it behind Annie's ear.

"You remembered," she whispered.

Too full to speak, he nodded. Then he got a shovel, and wrapping his arms around her from behind, they turned the first bit of earth in what would soon be the finest rose garden in the city.

And when the blue rose was in the ground, Colt turned Annie in his arms.

"This calls for a celebration," he said.

"Any ideas?"

"Maybe I'll think of something."

He swept her up and carried her to the rosewood bed, and there Colt pledged his love to his best friend, his wife, his Annie.

And afterward she lifted herself on her elbow and brushed his hair back from his forehead.

"Do you think we can make this a double celebration?" she said.

He couldn't resist teasing her. "We only planted one rosebush."

"We've planted more than a rosebush."

Until then he'd thought it wasn't possible to know more joy than on his wedding day. But this moment surpassed anything he'd ever dreamed of.

Tenderly he cupped his hands around the soft white mound of her belly.

"Annie, you've given me the greatest gift any man can hope for."

She reached onto the bedside table and plucked off a tiny greenware cup. Taking the blue rose, she pressed it into the wet clay.

"A symbol of our love," she whispered. "And when it goes through the fire, it will last always and forever."

EPILOGUE

Three people gathered around the hospital bed, admiring the child sleeping in Annie's arms—Colt wearing a smile as big as Texas, Pete vowing to pass out cigars to everybody, including the polo ponies, and Margaret sporting a sleek red bob and a diamond as big as a robin's egg.

"Isn't he the handsomest thing you've ever laid your eyes on?" Colt said.

"Anybody tries to tell me different, I'll hog-tie 'em and throw 'em into the bay."

"And I'll help you, Pete," Margaret said.

Everybody laughed at the idea of mild-mannered Margaret resorting to such uncivilized behavior. But then Margaret had been full of surprises lately, not the least of which was her announcement that she and Pete were getting married.

The tiny infant opened his eyes, and Annie pulled

the blanket back from his puckered pink face and held him up for another round of adoration.

"I can't wait for you to get out of here so I can baby-sit," Margaret said.

"Shoot, with this added attraction, I'm liable to have a hard time getting her to leave for a honeymoon." Pete stuck a finger into the baby's tiny fist, then grinned. "Heck, I might not want to leave, myself."

"Oh, you." Margaret punched him fondly in the ribs. Then she put her finger in the baby's other tiny fist. "What are you going to name him?"

Colt and Annie smiled at each other.

"Anthony," they said.

After everyone had gone, Colt and Annie lay in the narrow bed with their arms around each other. And outside in the winter-dark sky rose a single star, bigger than a baseball, casting its beam of light over the baby asleep in his crib.

THE EDITORS' CORNER

How often do you read a really good book? We hope that with LOVESWEPT, you read four. Per month. This month we're taking you on a trip around the country with four delightful romances from some of our best authors. From love on the range to the streets of New York and Dallas and the heart of the South, you're off on a journey of the heart.

The first gem is Marcia Evanick's **SILVER IN THE MOONLIGHT**, LOVESWEPT #906. Dean Warren Katz had nothing but the best of intentions when he wrote to Katherine Silver regarding the welfare of her aunts. He was just being neighborly to the little old ladies whose house was ready to cave in. When Katherine arrived in Jasper, South Carolina, it didn't take a genius to see that her aunts were hale and hearty. Now if she could just get her hands around Mr. Katz's neck. But he tells her to look below the surface, at the furniture placed to hide cracks in the walls, the broken shutters, not to mention the crumbling foundation, well hidden by a generous array of bushes. Sharing coffee, conversation, and a whole lot more, Dean and Katherine launch a crusade to renovate the house. Marcia Evanick's latest book is rich with romance, and highly reminiscent of mint juleps, old porches, rocking chairs, and, of course, starry southern nights.

RaeAnne Thayne returns with **SWEET JUSTICE**, LOVESWEPT #907. Somehow Nicholas Kincaid can't believe Ivy Parker when she says that he wouldn't even notice the 500 sheep she wants to raise on his land. Ivy's ranch is already dangerously close to bankruptcy, and without the fresh grass on Kincaid's land, she'll have to sell off part of the herd to buy food for the rest. Nick is her only hope, but all he wants is some peace and quiet. Lord knows he needs it—he's spent the past year trying the most-watched case since the O. J. Simpson trial. Nick's motto is Don't get involved, but when he learns how desperate Ivy's situation is, he relents. Now her problems are his as well, and suddenly, being neighbors isn't so bad. And as he watches Ivy stand her ground against the rumors and mysterious occurrences on the ranch, he realizes that in her he may have found the home he's never known. RaeAnne Thayne weaves a sensual and moving tale of passion and intrigue on the range.

Fayrene Preston tells us Kylie Damaron's story in **THE DAMARON MARK: THE LOVERS**, LOVESWEPT #908. Contrary to popular belief, you can go home again, and David Galado has done just that—much to Kylie's dismay. From the time she was a little girl, Kylie had depended on David to be her fierce protector from the dark shadows that had haunted her life. A chance encounter and misunderstandings had reduced them to mere acquaintances, a pretense that David had always tried to uphold. But when David learns of Kylie's new boyfriend, a man with dangerous connections, he can't stop himself from getting involved. Kylie's wondered a thousand times over about what would have happened if David had never left in the first place, and here's her chance to find out. But when an attempt on her life is made, will she allow herself to trust her heart and her future to a man she once thought she loved? Fayrene Preston answers that question when two lost souls throw fate to the wind and find solace in each other.

In **HOT PROPERTY,** LOVESWEPT #909, Karen Leabo pits a tough-talking detective against his awfully beautiful suspect. For Wendy Thayer, turning thirty is rough, but getting arrested on her birthday has got to take the cake. Despite all her objections to the contrary, Michael Taggart hauls Wendy into the station house on charges of transporting stolen goods. But the beautiful personal shopper insists that she and her favorite client are innocent of any wrongdoing. And once she's located Mr. Neff, she'll prove it, she promises. Wendy knows there's been a huge mistake, sweet Mr. Neff just couldn't be a criminal. But as Michael and Wendy search for the elusive old man, more clues keep popping up to incriminate Wendy. Michael has learned to distrust any woman who loves to spend money, never mind a woman who does it for a living. But when the odds are against them, will he gamble away his dreams for the chance to be with Wendy? In a delightful tale of passionate pursuit, Karen Leabo sends two unlikely lovers on a journey to discover their own unspoken longings.

Happy reading!

With warmest wishes,

Susann Brailey   *Joy Abella*

Susann Brailey   Joy Abella
Senior Editor   Administrative Editor

P.S. Look for these women's fiction titles coming in October! From *New York Times* bestselling author Iris Johansen comes **THE FACE OF DECEPTION**, the gripping story of a forensic sculptor who is hired to reconstruct a face from a skull—and is rewarded for her efforts with an odyssey of terror. In **MERELY MARRIED**, Patricia Coughlin presents a stunning love story set in Regency England, where a scandalous scheme backfires on a crafty rake who is determined to take himself off the marriage market. And from Ellen Fisher, an exciting new voice in historical romance, comes **THE LIGHT IN THE DARKNESS**. The last thing Edward Greyson expected was to be taken with Jennifer Leigh Chilton, who has transformed herself into the perfect light to shatter his darkness. Yet, until he can escape his troubled past, and the horrible secret that plagues his soul, he can never be free to love again. And immediately following this page, preview the Bantam women's fiction titles on sale in September.

For current information on Bantam's women's fiction, visit our website at the following address:
http://www.bdd.com/romance

Don't miss these extraordinary novels from Bantam Books!

On sale in September:

AND THEN YOU DIE
by Iris Johansen

WRITTEN IN THE STARS
by Katherine O'Neal

CHARMED AND DANGEROUS
by Jane Ashford

"Iris Johansen keeps the reader intrigued with complex characters and plenty of plot twists. The story moves so fast, you'll be reading the epilogue before you notice."—*People*

AND THEN YOU DIE

by *New York Times* bestselling author

Iris Johansen

Bess Grady had heard the unmistakable sound before. She knows what it means. But not even the eerie lament of the howling dogs can prepare her for what has taken place in the small village. The seasoned photojournalist had been sent there on an easy assignment, and now she has stumbled upon something she was never meant to see. Amid chaos and fear, she joins forces with an intimidating stranger, a man whose alliances are unclear but whose methods have a way of leaving bodies in his wake. For what she has witnessed is only the first stage in a plan of terror that may kill us all. And she has no choice but to stop it—or die trying. . . .

Holy Virgin, help them. Their immortal souls are writhing in Satan's fire.

Father Juan knelt at the altar, his gaze fixed desperately on the golden crucifix above him.

He had been in Tenajo for forty-four years and his flock had always listened before. Why would they not listen to him now in this supreme test?

He could hear them in the square outside the church, shouting, singing, laughing. He had gone out and told them they should be in their homes at this time of night, but it had done no good. They had only offered to share the evil with him.

He would not take it. He would stay inside the church.

And he would pray that Tenajo would survive.

"You slept well," Emily told Bess. "You look more rested."

"I'll be even more rested by the time we leave here." She met Emily's gaze. "I'm fine. So back off."

Emily smiled. "Eat your breakfast. Rico is already packing up the jeep."

"I'll go help him."

"It's going to be all right, isn't it? We're going to have a good time here."

"If you can keep yourself from—" Oh, what the hell. She wouldn't let this time be spoiled. "You bet. We're going to have a great time."

"And you're glad I came," Emily prompted.

"I'm glad you came."

Emily winked. "Gotcha."

Bess was still smiling as she reached the jeep.

"Ah, you're happy. You slept well?" Rico asked.

She nodded as she stowed her canvas camera case in the jeep. Her gaze went to the hills. "How long has it been since you've been in Tenajo?"

"Almost two years."

"That's a long time. Is your family still there?"

"Just my mother."

"Don't you miss her?"

"I talk to her on the phone every week." He frowned. "My brother and I are doing very well. We could give her a fine apartment in the city, but she would not come. She says it would not be home to her."

She had clearly struck a sore spot. "Evidently someone thinks Tenajo is a wonderful place or Condé Nast wouldn't have sent me."

"Maybe for those who don't have to live there. What does my mother have? Nothing. Not even a washing machine. The people live as they did fifty years ago." He violently slung the last bag into the jeep. "It is the priest's fault. Father Juan has convinced her the city is full of wickedness and greed and she should stay in Tenajo. Stupid old man. There's nothing wrong with having a few comforts."

He was hurting, Bess realized, and she didn't know what to say.

"Maybe I can persuade my mother to come back with me," Rico added.

"I hope so." The words sounded lame even to her. Great, Bess. She searched for some other way to help. "Would you like me to take her photograph? Maybe the two of you together?"

His face lit up. "That would be good. I've only a snapshot my brother took four years ago." He paused. "Maybe you could tell her how well I'm doing in Mexico City. How all the clients ask just for me?" He hurried on: "It would not be a lie. I'm very much in demand."

Her lips twitched. "I'm sure you are." She got into the jeep. "Particularly among the ladies."

He smiled boyishly. "Yes, the ladies are very kind to me. But it would be wiser not to mention that to my mother. She would not understand."

"I'll try to remember," she said solemnly.

"Ready?" Emily had walked to the jeep and was now handing Rico the box containing the cooking implements. "Let's go. With any luck we'll be in Tenajo by two and I'll be swinging in a hammock by four. I can't wait. I'm sure it's paradise on earth."

Tenajo was not paradise.

It was just a town baking in the afternoon sun. From the hilltop overlooking the town Bess could see a picturesque fountain in the center of the wide cobblestone plaza bordered on three sides by adobe buildings. At the far end of the plaza was a small church.

"Pretty, isn't it?" Emily stood up in the jeep. "Where's the local inn, Rico?"

He pointed at a street off the main thoroughfare. "It's very small but clean."

Emily sighed blissfully. "My hammock is almost in view, Bess."

"I doubt if you could nap with all that caterwauling," Bess said dryly. "You didn't mention the coyotes, Rico. I don't think that—" She stiffened. Oh, God, no. Not coyotes.

Dogs.

She had heard that sound before.

Those were dogs howling. Dozens of dogs. And their mournful wail was coming from the streets below her.

Bess started to shake.

"What is it?" Emily asked. "What's wrong?"

"Nothing." It couldn't be. It was her imagination. How many times had she awakened in the middle of the night to the howling of those phantom dogs?

"Don't tell me nothing. Are you sick?" Emily demanded.

It wasn't her imagination.

She moistened her lips. "It's crazy but— We have to hurry. *Hurry*, Rico."

Rico stomped on the accelerator, and the jeep careened down the road toward the village.

They didn't see the first body until they were inside the town.

He is her sworn enemy.
She is the prize he wants above all.

WRITTEN IN THE STARS

From the winner of the *Romantic Times* Award for
Best Sensual Historical Romance

Katherine O'Neal

"Katherine O'Neal continues to reign as the queen of romantic adventure."—*Affaire de Coeur*

Diana Sanbourne is faced with an impossible choice: ignore her father's dying wish or seek out the one man who can fulfill it. The one man she despises—Jack Rutherford. Once, she had loved him, only to be betrayed, and she vowed never again to fall under the power of his seductive caress. Now he's a rogue hunter of ancient relics, with the daring and instincts that could lead to the fabled treasure her father asked her to find. Yet even as he joins her on her quest—one that will lead from England's shadowy underworld to a treacherous distant land—Diana must guard not only her life but her heart. For Jack makes it clear he intends to reclaim her for his own. And she is just as determined not to surrender.

"So you want to find your father's bloody treasure, do you, Diana?" This wasn't the voice she remembered. It throbbed and seethed and demanded with all the passion she'd set loose. It stirred her deeply, causing her breath to come in wispy gasps. "His obsession with that treasure has destroyed my family and, I suspect, caused his own death. Would you like to see what it did to *me*?"

He jerked his jacket open and flung it, in one furious motion, across the room. Then he savagely ripped his shirt off, buttons scattering against the wooden floor, and sent it flying in the jacket's wake. As he did, Diana saw the criss-crossing of scars beneath the thick, dark hair and bronze expanse of his chest. His arms, sleekly muscled, were similarly scarred. When he turned his back to her she saw the faded tracks left by the cat-o'-nine-tails.

"Now tell me," he spat out, facing her again. "If my jailers couldn't break me, what makes you think I'd bend to your will?"

Her eyes had been riveted by the scars. Rather than deform him, they lent him the rugged, dashing quality of a martyr stoically holding his tongue beneath the most unimaginable torture. It actually made him more attractive, gave his finely honed body a sense of reckless adventure and romantic mystique.

Dragging her gaze back to his face, she said, "Because you owe me."

"I owe *you*? I'm the one who spent two lousy years in that hell-hole, wanting to die. I'm the one who had to wake up in the middle of the night to the sound of a turning key, knowing they were coming again, and wondering if I could take it one more time. *I'm* the one who didn't get so much as a *visit* from the woman who just two nights before had sworn to love me no matter what— If anything, baby, you owe *me*!"

She felt the outrage burst in her like a broken dam. "You insufferable boor! You wrested that promise from me under the falsest of pretenses. How could you have done that? To betray me so miserably after I gave you something I'd given no other man. I made *love* with you. I trusted you, Jack, with everything I had. And after all that, you didn't even have the decency to trust me with the truth. *Damn* you for what you did to us. If you rot in hell you can't make up for a *minute* of it."

That was why she hated him. That's why she'd do anything to see him on his knees before her.

But he wasn't on his knees. He was looking at her through a narrow, bitter gaze that spoke of his own betrayal at her hands. Yet it was the shrewd gaze of a quick mind ticking off the possibilities.

Jack remained as he was, stubbornly silent. There were things he hadn't told her, things that would help explain his actions. But now wasn't the time. He'd be damned if he gave her the satisfaction.

Diana straightened her shoulders, as if pulling together what was left of her dignity. His glance dropped to the out-thrust swell of her breasts.

"Tell me," he said, hooking one thumb beneath her jaw and lifting it to study her face. "Have you been with another man since our last encounter?"

"That's none of your concern," she snapped, jerking her chin away from his hand.

"No, but it would make the payment all the sweeter."

She narrowed her eyes. "What do you mean?"

"You want something from me. You've made it clear you'll stop at nothing. Should I leave now, no doubt you'll hound me until I tell you what you want to know. I hate to think what lengths you'll go to next. So the prudent thing would be to give in to your demands and be done with you once and for all. But that brings up the question of payment. You wouldn't expect to get something for nothing. And my services don't come cheaply, as you may know."

"Mercenaries never do."

"So, logically speaking, what have you to offer me?"

"Money," she said, a little too quickly.

"Money is of no use to me now. You don't have enough to make it interesting."

"What then?"

"What, indeed? What could you possibly have that would be worth my time?"

He was looking her up and down. "*Two minutes* of your time."

"Two years and two minutes," he corrected.

"That's not my fault."

"I'm a bitter man, Diana. I'm not ashamed to admit it. I despise you and your family every bit as much as you scorn me, if not more. I see it in your eyes that you want me punished for my sins. Well, guess what? I want you chastened just as much. So I ask myself, what could you possibly give me that would make your flesh crawl to hand over? What," he asked idly, tracing the back of his finger in a path from her collarbone to the soft mound of her breast, "indeed?"

She slapped his hand away. "If you think I'll stand still and let you blackmail me this way, you're madder than I thought."

"Cheeky words, coming from a kidnapper. We might as well be honest. We loved each other once, or thought we did, but we're adversaries now. We don't trust each other, and we each feel we have good reason. So any personal appeal you might make to me is guaranteed to fall on deaf ears. I'm on to you now, and am not bloody likely to fall prey to your trap a second time. I don't give a damn if you find your father's precious treasure. But since you do, here are my terms. I'll give you the information you want and you give me what you've—*given no other man.*"

"Jane Ashford is an exceptional talent."—*Rendezvous*

CHARMED AND DANGEROUS

by Jane Ashford

Gavin Graham works alone, trusts no one, and never, ever gives his heart. But the spy may have met his match in an ex-governess. Laura Devane has been handpicked to fulfill an important mission: distracting him from the deceptive charms of a Russian countess. Once, years ago, she defiantly rejected his marriage proposal. Now she meets his cool mockery and sensual advances with a maddening self-possession. And she plunges headlong into a perilous investigation that leaves him fearing for her safety. Clearly the woman is a menace—to international peace and to his peace of mind. For Laura's passion for intrigue matches his own, and her touch leaves him stunningly aroused, tempting him to join her in a life of dangerous desires. . . .

"You are looking very lovely this evening," said Gavin as he led Laura onto the dance floor at the Austrian embassy ball.

Startled, Laura looked up at him. It was the first compliment he had ever offered her, and she didn't trust it for a moment.

"That gown is unusual. But then, your clothes are all quite elegant."

She gazed down at the folds of her ball gown, fashioned of a silk that shimmered between bronze and deep green, depending on the light. She had been exceedingly pleased with the fabric and design from the moment she saw them. Looking at the gown now, she was filled with suspicion.

Gavin grasped her waist, and they began to dance, falling naturally, once again, into rhythm with each other. It was a waltz. Of course it was a waltz, Laura thought. A country dance or quadrille would offer him less scope to unsettle her.

"You're not usually so silent," commented Gavin, turning her deftly at the end of the room.

The strength of his arm was palpable, and his hands—on her back and laced with hers—held an unnerving heat. He was a man who demanded notice. You couldn't ignore him, and it would always be a serious mistake to discount him. At the same time, he made it terribly difficult to keep one's wits about one. It was a devastating combination. "Your coat is very well cut," she managed.

His eyes flickered, and one corner of his mouth turned up for a moment. "Thank you," he answered.

Evening dress did particularly become him, Laura mused. And he wore it with unmatched ease. She felt a flutter in her midsection, and wondered if her dinner was about to disagree with her.

"Having established that we are both creditably dressed, perhaps we could move on to some other topic," he added.

Always mocking, Laura thought. Did he speak seriously to anyone? To Sophie Krelov, perhaps? "Is Lord Castlereagh here tonight?" she asked him. "I haven't yet seen him."

"I believe so." Gavin turned his head to search for the chief of the English delegation at the congress. "He had planned to be."

"He must be eager not to offend the Austrians." Laura was also scanning the huge room.

"Indeed?"

Laura looked up at his surprised tone.

"And why should he be?" inquired Gavin.

"I assume he wants their support against Russia's demands."

"Has the general been educating you?" he said, with predictable irony.

"The general shares the common opinion that women understand nothing about politics," she responded tartly. "I believe he would sooner explain such matters to his horse."

"Oh, I think he would speak to the dog first."

Laura stared up at him, not sure she had heard correctly. A spurt of laughter escaped her.

"Where do you get your information, then?" he added.

"I am quite capable of reading."

"Reading?"

For some reason, the way he said the word made Laura recall the very unpolitical things she had read in the earl's private library. She flushed deep scarlet.

"Newspapers?" continued Gavin, looking fascinated at the reaction his remark had produced.

Unable to speak, she nodded.

"Perhaps not only the English papers? You seem to have a talent for languages."

"I have been reading all the accounts of the congress that I can find," she answered, regaining some measure of composure. "Hard as it may be for you to believe, I am deeply interested in what is going on here."

"It isn't at all hard for me to believe." His tone left Laura wondering whether he meant his words as an insult.

"It is oppressively warm in here, isn't it?" he remarked. In the next moment, he had led her into a tiny alcove and opened one of the French doors.

Then they were somehow through it and on a flagstone terrace that flanked the building. A large garden spread into darkness on their left. "There, that's better."

"Mr. Graham!" Laura struggled a little in his grasp. "Excuse me. I wish to go back in." It was quite unsuitable for them to be outside alone.

"But it is such a beautiful night," he argued, his arm adamant around her waist.

"On the contrary, it is quite chilly," she said, trying to step out of his grasp.

He swung her down two shallow steps into the garden. It was all Laura could do to keep her feet. Beyond the squares of light from the ballroom windows, the night was lit by a half moon, which turned the landscape into a maze of black and silver. Gavin swept her along to a row of shrubbery, inky masses against the stars, which Laura recognized only when their needles brushed her arm.

"Mr. Graham," she protested more loudly. "I ask you, as a gentleman, to—"

"You and the general make the same mistake in thinking I am a gentleman," he said. With a jerk, he pulled her tight against him, his lips capturing hers in a hard, inescapable kiss.

Laura stiffened in surprise and outrage. She pushed against his shoulders—with no effect. She wriggled and managed only to make herself even more conscious of the contours of his body melded to hers. She had never been in such intimate contact with anyone. One of his hands had slid well below her waist and was pressing her even closer. The muscles of his chest caressed her breasts in the most amazing way. And his lips moved confidently on hers, rousing sensations that she couldn't evade.

It was unthinkable. It was intolerable. It was

rather like some of the things she had read, Laura mused dizzily. One couldn't really understand, through mere words, how it felt, how one's whole being could suddenly turn traitor and melt like ice in a conflagration.

In the next instant, she was thrust away roughly and left swaying on her feet at arm's length.

"There," said Gavin unevenly.

Laura could see his face only dimly in the light from the distant windows. She thought for a moment that he looked almost shaken. But in the next, the sneering mockery was back.

"Was that what you wanted?" he said.

"I . . . ?"

"When you allowed me to bring you out here?"

"Allowed?"

"If the general suggested such a ploy, he is even denser than I realized."

"You practically dragged me out of the ballroom," Laura accused.

"Dragged? I think not." He said it in a caressing tone that made Laura's face go hot.

"You . . . you bastard."

"Tch. Is this language for a lady?"

Sweeping back her skirts, Laura kicked him in the shin. "Be thankful I am a lady," she said over her shoulder as she strode back toward the ball. "If I were not, that might have hurt a good deal more."

His derisive laughter followed her up the steps onto the terrace. Laura turned to glare at him, and he raised one finger in a lazy salute. Her fists clenched, and blood pounded through her temples. If she had had a pistol at that moment, she thought, she would have killed him.

On sale in October:

THE FACE OF DECEPTION
by Iris Johansen

MERELY MARRIED
by Patricia Coughlin

THE LIGHT IN THE DARKNESS
by Ellen Fisher

Bestselling Historical Women's Fiction

AMANDA QUICK

___ 28354-5 SEDUCTION . . . $6.50/$8.99 Canada
___ 28932-2 SCANDAL . . . . $6.50/$8.99
___ 28594-7 SURRENDER . . . . $6.50/$8.99
___ 29325-7 RENDEZVOUS . . . . $6.50/$8.99
___ 29315-X RECKLESS . . . . $6.50/$8.99
___ 29316-8 RAVISHED . . . . $6.50/$8.99
___ 29317-6 DANGEROUS . . . . $6.50/$8.99
___ 56506-0 DECEPTION . . . . $6.50/$8.99
___ 56153-7 DESIRE . . . . $6.50/$8.99
___ 56940-6 MISTRESS . . . . $6.50/$8.99
___ 57159-1 MYSTIQUE . . . . $6.50/$8.99
___ 57190-7 MISCHIEF . . . . $6.50/$8.99
___ 57407-8 AFFAIR . . . . $6.99/$8.99

IRIS JOHANSEN

___ 29871-2 LAST BRIDGE HOME . . . $5.50/$7.50
___ 29604-3 THE GOLDEN
             BARBARIAN . . . . $6.99/$8.99
___ 29244-7 REAP THE WIND . . . . . $5.99/$7.50
___ 29032-0 STORM WINDS . . . . . . $6.99/$8.99

Ask for these books at your local bookstore or use this page to order.

Please send me the books I have checked above. I am enclosing $____ (add $2.50 to cover postage and handling). Send check or money order, no cash or C.O.D.'s, please.

Name _____

Address _____

City/State/Zip _____

Send order to: Bantam Books, Dept. FN 16, 2451 S. Wolf Rd., Des Plaines, IL 60018
Allow four to six weeks for delivery.
Prices and availability subject to change without notice.

Bestselling Historical Women's Fiction

⚜ IRIS JOHANSEN ⚜

___ 28855-5 THE WIND DANCER ...$5.99/$6.99
___ 29968-9 THE TIGER PRINCE ...$6.99/$8.99
___ 29944-1 THE MAGNIFICENT
            ROGUE ....$6.99/$8.99
___ 29945-X BELOVED SCOUNDREL .$6.99/$8.99
___ 29946-8 MIDNIGHT WARRIOR ..$6.99/$8.99
___ 29947-6 DARK RIDER ....$6.99/$8.99
___ 56990-2 LION'S BRIDE ......$6.99/$8.99
___ 56991-0 THE UGLY DUCKLING...$6.99/$8.99
___ 57181-8 LONG AFTER MIDNIGHT.$6.99/$8.99
___ 57998-3 AND THEN YOU DIE....$6.99/$8.99

⚜ TERESA MEDEIROS ⚜

___ 29407-5 HEATHER AND VELVET .$5.99/$7.50
___ 29409-1 ONCE AN ANGEL .....$5.99/$7.99
___ 29408-3 A WHISPER OF ROSES .$5.99/$7.99
___ 56332-7 THIEF OF HEARTS ...$5.50/$6.99
___ 56333-5 FAIREST OF THEM ALL .$5.99/$7.50
___ 56334-3 BREATH OF MAGIC ...$5.99/$7.99
___ 57623-2 SHADOWS AND LACE ..$5.99/$7.99
___ 57500-7 TOUCH OF ENCHANTMENT.$5.99/$7.99
___ 57501-5 NOBODY'S DARLING ..$5.99/$7.99

Ask for these books at your local bookstore or use this page to order.

Please send me the books I have checked above. I am enclosing $____ (add $2.50 to cover postage and handling). Send check or money order, no cash or C.O.D.'s, please.

Name _____

Address _____

City/State/Zip _____

Send order to: Bantam Books, Dept. FN 16, 2451 S. Wolf Rd., Des Plaines, IL 60018
Allow four to six weeks for delivery.
Prices and availability subject to change without notice.

FN 16 9/98